I0683250

Tales of Toratoga:

THE BOY WITH NINE FINGERS

BY NICK LYON

Tales of Toratoga: The Boy with Nine Fingers

By Nick Lyon

Cover design by Nick Lyon

Printed in the United States of America by CreateSpace

ISBN: 0615487629
ISBN-13: 978-0615487625

For A.B.

Who inspires me to dance,

To write,

And to love.

CONTENTS

Chapter 1

The Old House

The once good and great king sat in his castle, planning the destruction of his opposing forces, while somewhere, worlds apart, was a boy with nine fingers, standing in the front yard of his new house. At that moment, the boy knew nothing of the king's existence, and the king only heard a passing rumor of the boy's. But they would know each other soon.

The sun rose, glancing off the golden heads of wheat, dancing with the wind out in the fields that stretched on and on around the edges of Abbey, Oklahoma. By 9:30 that morning, the temperature had already reached a stifling 87 degrees and was well over 100 degrees by noon. The only people out on the streets in that afternoon heat were the young boys out seeking adventures, which they could almost always find. Only young boys were out, save one.

The mayor of Abbey, Oklahoma, was walking his way down to 1223 Ash Street. His navy suit absorbed the heat very well, causing his body heat to rise tremendously. Despite the fact that sweat stood out on his large forehead, the mayor smiled and hummed slightly as he walked. Two new people had moved into his town, and Abbey's small size allowed him to easily keep track of the new residents. So he always made it a point to stop by the house, introduce himself, and attempt to make the new people feel welcome.

Mayor Hank Walton, or "Boss," as everyone called him, had a round face with a rounder belly that hung out over his waist like a death-defying cliffhanger. He was a cheerful man and was voted mayor by default, as he was the only one to run. Most people in Abbey thought that Boss did a fine job, and that's the way things should stay, at least as long as he was able to be the mayor.

Boss reached the small yellow house on Ash Street, which was only three blocks from his own, and found a small boy standing out in the lawn of the yard.

"Hello there," Boss called when he stepped into the yard.

The boy looked at him curiously, but didn't say anything.

"I said hello there." This time Boss extended his hand to shake the boy's.

The boy reluctantly stuck his hand out and allowed the chubby man to take it. They shook briefly, and the boy continued to look at the newcomer with sparkling blue eyes. Boss felt a slim uneasiness work its way through him as he looked into those eyes. He felt they could search his very soul.

"Well, my name is Hank Walton, mayor of this fine city." No matter how small the town was, the residents always felt a need to call it a city. "Folks 'round here call me Boss, which I guess would be just fine if that's what you'd like to call me. And what do they call you?"

2

"My name is Jacob Kepler," the boy answered.

"Ah, yes, Jacob, so your mother must be Mary-Anne?"

Jacob nodded.

"And it's just the two of you?"

Jacob nodded again.

"Well, what do you think of Abbey so far?"

Jacob shrugged his shoulders, looked to his right then to his left, seemed to spot something he found interesting and said, "It's all right, I guess. Some neat houses."

"Why, yes, there are, and we also have some good restaurants as well." Boss patted his tummy. "I maybe partake in the local food establishments more than I should, but they taste so fine. Right, well, give your mother my card." He handed Jacob his blue and white business card, "Let her know that I came by. Can you do that, son?"

"Sure."

"Okay, well, I should get back." He took a hanky out of his pocket and attempted to mop the excess water off of his large face, clearly looking forward to getting back to the air-conditioning of his house. "It sure was a pleasure to meet you." He extended his hand again and shook Jacob's before walking off, never noticing that the boy was missing his right index finger.

Jacob stood in front of his house for a few more minutes watching the round mayor walk back down the street. "Boss," he said with a smile, thinking that the man really enjoyed being called such a silly name. He tore the business card into small pieces and dropped them, letting the strong Oklahoma wind carry the shredded card away.

3

He didn't like living in Abbey very much, though it was where he and his mother finally planted their belongings. They'd looked everywhere between Woodson, Texas, to Kimble, Nebraska, but his mother could find no suitable employment. But she wanted to live in the Great Plains.

He stood there on the street in front of his house looking around, taking in his new neighborhood, noticing again and again the large house at the end of the street. He'd lived in Abbey for three days, and he couldn't get used to it. He missed his dad and his brother Taylor terribly; besides, this didn't really feel like home to him.

The missing finger on his right hand was the only thing that Jacob felt made him special, despite his mother's insistences that he was a "very unique young man". He lost his finger a couple months before his parents split up, and somehow, he felt responsible for the demise of their relationship. Like their marriage only lasted as long as their children had all their limbs.

He was lonely, and while he didn't want to admit it, he wasn't too sure he had any other choice. He'd left all of his friends, including his brother Taylor, back in South Carolina, where very few people lived, and everyone knew why he and his mother no longer lived there. Rumors fly fast in those small towns. Because of his loneliness, Jacob invited Taylor into his mind, so that even though Taylor was a thousand miles away, he could hear his brother's voice in his mind as though he were with him all the time. It wasn't quite the same as living with Taylor, but it was better than living without him completely.

There was no point in wasting his time thinking about his old life now, though; he had to get started on a new one. With his mother beginning her new job at the nursing home that day, he had plenty of time to go out and explore the interesting parts of Abbey, Oklahoma.

So far, he'd learned that the population of Abbey was slightly more than 6,000, and to him, that was a city, allowing him to fit in with the townspeople more than he knew. Growing up in a town of 700 people, one found that anything larger seemed huge.

He looked down to the end of Ash Street. Three blocks down from his little two-bedroom yellow house, the street ended abruptly at that large house that continued to catch his eye. He loved the stories of knights and kingdoms, of Arthur and Lancelot, and to Jacob, that house looked like a castle where dragons might be trying to attack the great king or where the Green Knight might show up to challenge one of Arthur's knights. Jacob fell in love with the house as soon as they pulled up to their own. That's where he would like to live if he could. He asked his mom about it as soon as she put the car in park three days earlier.

"Jacob, I don't like the looks of that place. I'll trust you to not go wandering around up there."

"Ah, but, Mom. Look at it, it's incredible."

"Remember, you don't have an older brother to lead you into trouble anymore."

At the mention of Taylor, Jacob shut up and looked at his hands.

The once beautiful home at the end of Ash Street now featured chipped paint on the wood trim, worn shingles, overgrown hedges, and a lawn that was mowed only three times during the summer. Brown brick and black rock decorated the outside walls, giving it that castle appearance. It was great as far as houses are concerned, and to Jacob's young mind, there was no greater house built by man.

The Taylor in his mind loved the house even more than he. *We have to go up there for a look around,* Make-Believe-Taylor said.

"We don't have to," Jacob replied. "Besides, you heard what Mom said."

Come on, you like it. Let's just go. It won't take a minute. Mom won't even know.

"Taylor, I don't think that's the best idea."

You never do, but you always have fun anyway.

Taylor had a way of convincing him to do anything, especially before he was only a voice in Jacob's mind. He realized people would probably think it strange that he stood around having conversations with a brother that wasn't there, but Jacob didn't mind. People do strange things when they're lonely to try to get over the loneliness.

He walked the three blocks, sweating under the sun but not caring because that's what boys do: sweat and get dirty. He knew in the back of his mind, though, that his mother would probably make him take a bath that evening. She usually made him when he'd been outside all day. He walked on anyway.

Finally he reached the house's front lawn and stared, taking in everything that would fit into his small eyes. The house itself was two stories tall, with a very large attic on the third. The architectural ingenuity of the porch welcomed visitors with two pillars on either side of the great front doors, which were twice the size of normal doors so it looked as if a giant lived there. The house sat back on a sea of grass that parted for a sidewalk that was cracked and looked as if it wouldn't last much longer in the tidal waves of weeds that rose up around it. Ash Street, on which Jacob was still standing, ended in the large driveway that flowed right up to the house's three-car garage to the left.

He reached down and felt the remains of a ring in his pocket, as he often did during times of nervousness. The bent and twisted ring was now his good luck charm after its whole form had brought him such bad luck. He smiled as he thought about the day his dad had given him the ring. "Now take good care of that, Jacob, I've had that ring for a long time," his dad had said. He'd tried to take care of the ring, but the metal couldn't hold under the strain of his weight.

He took one look behind him to make sure no one was watching and made his decision. He stepped off the road onto the sidewalk that came right down next to the road. As soon as he was standing on the sidewalk, the cement under his feet finally gave up its fight against the grass. Jacob screamed, but to no avail. He sank down into the tide of green that swept him away. He lost sight of the house and Ash Street, the grass swallowed his body whole, and dirt filled his mouth and nose blocking all airflow. He triumphantly thrust one arm through the grass, but the grass swelled around it, and all hope of escape was snuffed out. He became a part of the lawn.

Jacob blinked the image away.

Who's afraid of grass?

"Shut up, Taylor," he said. He walked up the sidewalk to the front steps of the house. As his breathing quickened, and the fear began to grip him, Jacob missed his brother.

Back in South Carolina, Taylor, who was two years older than Jacob, had kept him out of trouble, as well as *in* it from time to time. Once, they'd ridden their bikes out to the graveyard that was haunted, at least it was according to the folklore around the town. Jacob didn't want to go, but it didn't take much for Taylor to convince him to do whatever he wanted. They went and while there, a spooky old man climbed out from behind a tombstone and began yelling incoherently at the boys. In one hand, he waved a brown paper bag, while the other pointed at the tombstone he'd just crawled from. The boys wasted no time and bolted immediately. Once they got home, their mother got the story from them. They were grounded for a week for riding that far from home without permission. She didn't even care that they'd seen a ghost of an old man.

Thinking back on that now, Jacob smiled again. Memories of his brother were comforting, and while thinking of him, he slowly took his hand away from the remains of the ring in his pocket.

Jacob finally stopped walking when he reached the massive porch on the front of the house. He counted five steps, before looking back over his shoulder one more time, and hesitantly, climbed the steps to the porch.

In brighter days, the porch would have been wonderful for sitting with neighbors, with family, with friends, watching the end of the day, having a cookout, telling ghost stories. Now, the porch had a strange death look that gave Jacob a slight shiver. A pile of dead leaves lay in the corner of the porch, blown there relentlessly by the wind. The once tan brick of the porch now looked black and dirty, like hands of a gravedigger. There was one long bench on the porch, the paint chipping off of it in little flakes. The exposed wood on the bench was black and rotted.

No one's lived here for a long time.

"Yeah, I see that," Jacob said.

He placed his left hand on one of the wooden pillars that also showed its wear from facing the elements. Jacob imagined himself living here with his mom and dad and Taylor during happier times when his parents got along. He could see himself sitting with his brother on the bench, Taylor telling him a story that would keep him from sleeping soundly that night. His mother would be inside cooking supper for them, and his dad would be riding a mower around the yard. The thought was pleasant and gave Jacob one more smile before he faced the house again.

He tipped his head all the way back to take in the entire door.

You have to try to open it, Jacob, Make-Believe-Taylor said.

"Yeah, I know."

He gave the handle on the door a gentle tug. It was locked. He suspected that much and breathed a small sigh of relief because he was right. He didn't really want to go into the house to look around, but the Taylor in his mind kept encouraging him.

He jumped from the side of porch and wandered around to the back of the house. Large hedges ran all along the side of the house, probably to keep people from getting too close, Jacob guessed. The hedges were overgrown and not taken care of. Whoever gardened here certainly had taken a break from it for a while.

The gigantic backyard of the old house ended in a wall composed of the same rock and brick of the house. Two large trees stood in the middle of the yard, close enough to each other to create a canopy with their branches. The sun couldn't pry its way through the branches of the tree to hit the ground below it, so there was a bare dirt patch all around the trees. Jacob decided this looked like a great place to relax.

He sat and rested his back against the trunk of one tree. He felt the cool breeze blow in the shade of the trees and felt suddenly sleepy. The sun was powerless under those trees. He stared up at the back of the house where the attic window rested just below the peak of the house. It was one of those small round windows he'd seen in movies of really large houses. Looking at that window, he thought he could see someone looking back at him.

"That has to be my imagination," he said.

Yeah, but it really does look like someone is there, doesn't it? Make-Believe-Taylor said.

Jacob's eyes were growing heavier, "I suppose, Taylor."

Well, don't just sit there. Get up and knock on the door. Get them to let us inside.

"Yeah, I will in a minute. I just want to rest a little."

Taylor tried to protest, but Jacob's mind was already shutting down, and with his mind went Taylor.

The imaginary person Jacob thought he saw in the window, as it turned out, was not so imaginary, and as he drifted off to sleep, a small girl came wandering out the back door of the house for a closer look at Jacob. She had long blond hair that stretched almost down to her feet. Her eyes were violet and slanted slightly upward, and the tops of her ears peaked out of her hair like the morning sun breaking from the horizon. The most peculiar thing about this girl, however, was not the way she looked, but the way she was dressed.

10

She wore a long, dark green robe that kept her feet hidden. It was decorated with black trim at the neck and wrists. On her right hand, she wore a silver ring with intricate designs and a stone in the center that matched her robe. Her robe was a silky material that was light and graceful, yet warm and tough. She was not dressed for June in Oklahoma.

Yet the heat seemed not to bother her. She walked through the shadows of the two trees to get a closer look at the boy, for a boy was all he was, she realized. She stayed light on her feet, trying not wake up Jacob from his sleep, but one wrong step and he was up.

His eyes popped open and darted from side to side to look for whatever it was that made the sound. He'd fallen asleep under a tree in the backyard of the old house, yes, he remembered that much. Then he remembered the face up in the window, it must not have been his imagination after all. He froze then, his mind throwing crazy ideas in his head of what could be watching him.

He saw just a flash of green through the shadow of the trees. His breath quickened, and not for the last time, he wished his brother was with him.

"Who's there?" he finally broke the silence with the question.

Although he hoped against a response, he got one.

"My name is Alice," an unfamiliar voice said.

Of course it's unfamiliar, Make-Believe-Taylor said. *You're new around here, remember?*

"Alice? Where are you?" he said.

"I am in the tree above you, Jacob."

He was startled by the use of his name. He knew then that this must be his overactive imagination, and he knew that when he looked up, he wouldn't see anyone.

But he did see someone. A small girl who looked only slightly older than him, with purple eyes and pointed ears. He almost fainted with surprise but regained control of himself.

"Why, hello," he said, his voice trembling only a little.

"Hi."

"How did you know my name?"

Alice paused to think about his question. "Well," she said finally. "I know all about you, Jacob. I need you to come back into my world with me, to help me save it. You're our only hope."

This time, Jacob, too overwhelmed by the heaviness of this news, fainted.

Chapter 2

Alice

It was ten minutes before Alice could wake Jacob. She now sat on the ground next to him, gently rubbing his face. He felt the metal of the ring gliding across his flesh.

His eyes fluttered open.

"Oh, there you are, Jacob."

He slowly sat up. She sat looking intently at him; her purple eyes almost seemed to glow in the shadows of the tree, complimenting the strange glow of Jacob's blue ones. Jacob saw that she was beautiful.

"How old are you?" he asked.

"Age has no importance right now, Jacob."

"What did you say your name was?"

"My name is Alice, and yours is Jacob. Now, I must tell you the reason I am here."

"Uh, okay. Is this really real, Alice? I mean, are you real?"

"Real?" She laughed, a beautiful sparkly sound. "Of course I'm real, Jacob. As real as you or that tree you've been sleeping under. I come from a land called Toratoga."

"How did you get here?" Jacob looked around for some sort of space craft, but saw none.

"I used a portal to cross into your world. Few of them still exist between our lands, but they can be found. One happens to be in the attic of this old house."

"And are there others like you?"

"Yes, of course. I am an Orn-child. We live in the Goldwood Forest. I come from the Treetop City at the heart of the forest. It is the central location for all of Orn life. Other townships reside in the forest, but none as immaculate as the Treetop City."

"You live in trees?"

"Well, yes. In better times, my people could talk to the trees, and the trees would respond by giving us homes in their boughs. Some communities have formed on the ground, but most have been abandoned for higher ground."

"Why? Is it dangerous now?"

"Yes. A shadow has fallen on the land, and now there are constant raids into our forest to slaughter my people and my kinsmen, the Elves."

"Elves?" The idea was incredible to Jacob, but he decided to continue the conversation rather than focus on the Elves. "What hunts you?"

"It's King Ro, a human king. Evil has taken hold of him and twisted him into the most dangerous mad man our land has ever known. He leads the humans against us and even called forth the Grebbles from across the Great Sea.

"The Grebbles are a magnificent creature. Their beauty cannot be surpassed by any. Their skin is a beautiful shade of blue, and they have long white hair that causes envy in any female. And their scent is sweeter than any flower we have in Toratoga. It is intoxicating and most people who smell it want it more. Once a person gets close enough to the Grebbles, however, there is another aroma under the first. This stench is worse than rotting flesh and soured blood. When you smell that, it's too late for you. You've been caught.

"But don't let their beautiful exteriors fool you. They are cruel and monstrous. They are powerful enough to rip your arms and legs from your body without any effort at all. Their speed and agility mark them as one of the most dangerous species in our entire world. The legend is that they descended from the sky, because the sky was jealous of the earth. The Grebbles were formed to destroy the earth's inhabitants to bring glory to the sky. I believe that is why they retain their color."

Jacob's mind burned with the details of the story Alice spilled out for him. He wondered briefly if all of it could possibly be real, but he pushed the thought away as Alice continued. The fact that he was a boy helped him believe in the story as all little boys believe that one day they will perform magic and fight evil. It wasn't a question of if, but only when.

"King Ro, the once good and great king, let evil overrun him after he found his wife with another lover. King Ro murdered his wife and her lover and a blackness settled over the land, stealing away the color of our world. It arose slowly like a strange fog, but the more evil deeds King Ro and his followers did, the more the blackness overtook our land. Even the sun cannot penetrate the evil, leaving the land cold and dull.

"Even the magic has forsaken us."

"What happened to the magic?"

"With the fall of King Ro, the magic in Toratoga failed. The trees and other elements of Toratoga that hold the secrets to magic refuse now to relinquish it to any. The trees have even stopped talking to the Orns.

"The land of Toratoga is being destroyed daily from the inside out. The evil that King Ro brought upon us is killing it. Now, there is very little color in Toratoga. Colored items are so rare that the humans use them to demonstrate wealth. The only species to remain its true form are the Grebbles. This is my first time to see the old color of my clothes in ages." She paused for a moment to admire the greens of her robe.

"Jacob," she continued, "evil should never have entered Toratoga. Because King Ro chose his evil path, the once beautiful provinces are now but a shadow of their once great glory. Great trees of the Goldwood Forest turned to sand, creating a vast gray desert.

"The King's evil seems to grow daily, and his raids into the forest are killing my people."

"Do the humans follow the king?"

"King Ro himself is of the human race. The humans side with him because of their natural desire for evil. Some of the human soldiers have risked their destruction and joined us in the fight."

"But how can I save you? I'm only a kid. I could barely find the courage to even walk up to this house." Jacob's emotions came out in a rush. He was suddenly very afraid.

16

"I know, but you did. You hesitated, but you found the courage you needed. You overcame your fears. You did it once, and you can do it again."

"You're talking about war. War! You are comparing dying on a battlefield to walking up to a house."

"Jacob, just because the subject is different, that doesn't mean the courage to overcome it is anything less. No matter what the courage needed is, you will find you have it."

He considered this then remembered one of the most curious problems with this conversation. "How do you know my name?"

Alice looked down at the ground and thought about her answer. "One of the Tribesmen. Elda is her name. She had the ability to see the future long before any of this happened. She foresaw the state of Toratoga as it is now. And she prophesied a savior for our world. She wrote everything she saw down in a book that is only known to the Orns. She wrote about Jacob, Jacob with nine fingers, who would come to our land and save our people from the ruling of King Ro."

He looked down at his right hand. He wiggled the stub where his index finger should have been. He still remembered the pain of losing it. "But I just lost my finger a few months ago. How could it be me?"

"I didn't expect a boy when I first came. I had the idea of a warrior in mind. One that would lead the Orns into battle to triumph over King Ro. But here you are."

"I don't think you have the right person."

"But it must be you, Jacob. There is no coincidence that I would find you outside the portal on this day and you are missing a finger. Tell me how you lost it."

17

He looked at her, startled by the demand. Everyone in is hometown knew about it; when a siren wails through a town of 700 people, everyone finds out why. He wasn't used to people asking about it. "In my old town, me and my brother, Taylor, were out goofing off. Back then I used to wear my dad's ring. It was silver with a green stone in the middle. I loved it.

"Anyway, Taylor dared me to go up on the roof of our house. We had a fairly large house, with a very steep roof. From the ground, it didn't look like that big of a deal, but once I got there, it was awful. I could barely stand up, until finally, my feet slipped out from under me. There was nothing to stop me from falling off. My jeans tore, and my hands were skinned from the shingles.

"At the edge of the roof, I finally caught hold, but not with my hand. It was with my ring. I hung there from the edge of the roof, dangling by my finger until my brother could get the ladder over to me to get me down. My finger swelled, and it finally gave up right when my feet touched the ladder. It just broke right off, ring and all. It was the worst pain I'd ever felt. The pressure bent the ring beyond repair. But I still carry it in my pocket."

"Did your ring look like this?" Alice lifted her right index finger to him, showing the silver ring.

He stared at it. There was no mistaking that it was an exact replica of his father's ring.

"How did you find that?"

"These are the gifts of the Northern Orns, the cave dwellers. They mine the stones, and build the rings with magic. Well, at least they did. Few Orns are given the rings, and now, without magic, we've lost contact with the Northern Orns. They've locked themselves into their caves and refuse to open them, and the road to the mountains is very dangerous. Few Orns have made it and lived. Maybe your father visited Toratoga and got one. Maybe it's just a coincidence."

Jacob nearly collapsed in his effort to believe the story. This girl turned up in the middle of his nap with an exact replica of his ring on the same finger he just lost. He knew this was all something in his head, like the voice of his brother. His imagination was too active at times.

"So here you are, Jacob, a boy with nine fingers, waiting to save a world quite different from your own."

"I don't think I'm quite ready to save anything yet."

"I don't expect you to be ready now that I see you. You are just a boy, but the Orn Warriors can train you. You will be welcomed as a king, once they see what you can do."

"Oh...what? Do? What can I do?"

"*Magic*, Jacob."

"Magic? I can't do magic."

"Here? No, you can't, but in Toratoga, you can. There is magic in my world, and you will find that you have the power to wield it. According to Elda's prophecy, you will be able to use magic and save us. The trees will respond to you."

"But, I just don't see how that's possible, Alice."

"All you have to do is come with me through the portal, and you will see everything. You will know what it means to be a hero."

"So you want me to come into your world right now, leave everything I know here behind, and attempt to save you?"

"Yes."

"Wait, what time is it?" Jacob looked at his watch and saw that it was five minutes past five. He gasped. "I have to get home. My mom will kill me if she finds out I've been up here."

"Wait, Jacob, you're our only hope." Her purple eyes fell with sorrow.

"I know. Wait for me, and I will come. I promise, but first I have to say goodbye to my mom. I don't know when I'll see her again."

Alice's face darkened, but she nodded. "I will wait for you. Goodbye, Jacob."

"Goodbye, Alice."

Jacob ran all the way home. He got there just as his mother did. He stole one more glance toward the old house before rushing up to the car to talk to his mom.

Chapter 3

The Bathtub

His mother got out of the car, wearing blue scrubs and looking at him in that peculiar way, like she knew he'd been up to something.

"You haven't been up to that house, have you?" she asked as she walked up the sidewalk to meet him.

"You told me not to."

"Yes, I know, Jacob, but you've done a lot of things I told you not to do in the past."

"Well, yeah, I went up there for a look around."

Mary-Anne's eyes widened and her eyebrows arched high onto her forehead at hearing her son tell her the truth so easily. Then her eyes narrowed, face reddened, and her nostrils flared. "Get in the house right now." Her low voice sounded stern enough for Jacob to act without arguing.

His strange meeting with Alice continued to replay through his mind and thoroughly threw his world into a frenzy. His mother followed him in, and he knew what was coming. He'd done enough stupid things with his brother to know that his mother was going to yell until her face turned an alarming purple color. He thought of his room and how much time he would be spending there for the next few weeks. Forget about lands of adventure, he would be grounded for sure.

"While I was at work, I was talking to one of my co-workers, and she told me the secret behind that house."

Not for the first time that day, Jacob felt surprise. The anger his mother showed in the yard was gone. "What happened up there, Mom?" His curiosity of the house got the better of him, but still he watched his mother cautiously.

"It seems that about ten years ago, a Mr. Hanson bought the house and moved in with his wife. His wife died a few months later, and Mr. Hanson was never the same. He went around spending all of his life's money on antiques. The people in town thought he was crazy.

"Then about three years ago, he disappeared. No one knows what happened to him, but he must have been expecting it. He set up some people to take care of things while he was gone, and if he wasn't back after three years, they could do whatever they wanted with the house."

Jacob stared at her, emotions rampaging inside his body. He didn't know what to say. He wondered briefly if this could have anything to do with Toratoga, but now that he was away from the old house and away from Alice, it didn't seem as real as it once did.

"So, this guy disappeared?"

"Yeah, and at the end of this year, the people he picked to take care of things around there own the house. So the house has a prospect of new owners, and I don't want you running around in their yard making them angry. Please, Jacob, just listen this once."

"Yeah, sure, Mom. What's for supper?" She gave him her trademark smile, and he loved her in spite of the discipline that Taylor hated so much.

"It will be ready in about an hour. Why don't you go watch some TV or something, while I start cooking?"

"Okay."

Jacob walked back through the kitchen, down the short hall, to his room. He lay on his bed staring at the ceiling. It had been a few hours since he'd heard from Taylor, so he sat waiting on his brother's input. Finally he spoke.

You'd better get up there soon before Alice leaves without you.

"Taylor, I'm not too sure I want to go back up there. What if it was all a trick played by my mind?"

I was there, too, and I saw Alice, and I heard what she had to say.

"You're in my mind. I made you up."

Yes, but you still talk to me and consider what I think.

"So you think we should walk back up Ash Street, climb into some portal, and attempt to save some world we've never heard of?"

Yeah, exactly. You'd be the hero. Instead of sitting in here and imagining all the glory and fame in the world, you could actually get it.

It was true that Jacob imagined a lot of glory and fame for himself. He dreamed of being a famous baseball player for the Yankees, but he also wanted to be a big rock star. He never could make up his mind on that subject.

"I want fame and glory in my own world."

Fine, when you get back you can write a book on your adventures in Toratoga.

"Now, there's a thought."

Jacob's mind then began to pursue the thought of capturing glory and fame as a writer. A writer who saved Toratoga from the destructive ruling of the evil King Ro. "But what if it's not real?"

It would still make a good story.

He was lost in his thoughts of writing when his mother called after him, "Jacob, dinner's ready."

He went into the kitchen where they'd set up a small table and two chairs for them to have a place to eat. "I want us to eat together as a family," his mom had said when she bought the table and chairs. Jacob had no arguments. He liked eating with his mother. And he didn't point out that they were only part of a family.

He sat down at the table and looked upon a tater-tot casserole with green beans on the side. "Green beans, Mom?"

"Yes, and you're going to eat every one of them. Don't think I have forgotten what you did today."

He began to plow the food into his mouth, the overwhelming concerns of an impossible land running through his head. He wanted so much for it to be real. At the very least, he wanted to see Alice again.

His mother, having eaten many meals with him, noticed a change in his behavior, and like all good mothers do, commented on it.

"Jacob, what's bugging you?" He continued to eat, not noticing his mother's concern. She got through to him on the second try.

"Oh, nothing, Mom. Why?"

"Well, you're quiet and you're just shoving your food in your mouth like you haven't eaten in days. You never act like that."

"I'm sorry, Mom."

"Sorry for what? Are you going to tell me what's wrong?"

Without even stopping to consider the outcome of telling her such things, he spilled it all to her. He told her about waking up to meet Alice, how their rings were exactly the same, and how he was supposed to save Toratoga from King Ro. He told her of his worries about whether the land was real or not. His mother sat listening intently, and when he was finally finished, she put her fork down.

"That sounds like a fun game, Jacob. I wish Taylor were here to play it with you," she finally said.

"So you think it's a game? It seemed so real when I was up there."

At this, Jacob's mother took a turn for the worse, and he realized he'd made a mistake telling her about it. Her voice wrenched the thoughts of Toratoga from him.

"I don't want to hear you talk about this again, Jacob. I don't want you pretending that there is some other world existing out there," she said, her voice rising with each word. Jacob didn't know what to say, he'd only heard his mother yell like this at his dad, and that was only when things were really bad.

He lowered his head and stared at the table while his mother continued to rant. He wasn't so sure he believed anymore, and even if he did, he sure didn't want to. He looked back up at his mom, and she finally shut up when she saw his eyes full of tears that danced on the edge of his eyelid before spilling down his cheeks. She stood from her seat, and crossed to his side of the table. She hugged him.

He loved his mother. At times, he blamed her for the separation between his dad and brother, but he didn't really understand all the circumstances. He realized it could have been just as much his dad's fault as his mom's. He quit thinking about it and just relished in the hug his mother gave him.

He went to his room after dinner, trying to concentrate on anything but Toratoga. He didn't want to make his mother angry again, so he began to clean his room. Before he got started, however, his mother's voice carried down the hall to his room. But she wasn't talking to him.

"Ryan, did you ever tell Jacob about your fantasy land?" He heard her say. Apparently she was on the phone with his father. "You didn't?" She continued. "It's nothing. He just mentioned something earlier that reminded me of it. No, you don't need to talk to him. No, he's in his room." She sighed. "Just forget about it, Ryan. Goodbye."

Jacob stared at the door of his bedroom for a minute, trying to understand what he'd just overheard. He remembered Alice suggesting that maybe his father had visited her world. His heart began to beat rapidly. It suddenly seemed more realistic than it had since he'd met Alice.

That night, Jacob was in bed staring at the ceiling when his mother came into the room.

"Hey, Jacob."

"Hey, Mom, what's up?"

"I wanted to talk to you about what you said earlier. I'm really sorry I snapped at you." She came to his bed and wrapped her arms around him. "Your father used to mumble about some strange things like that in his sleep

26

sometimes, and I thought for a minute that you knew that. I thought you were trying to blame me in some terrible way for your father and me splitting up." She began to cry as she held him.

"I'm sorry I ever brought it up, Mom, I had no idea." She turned and walked out of his room without another word, still struggling with the tears.

He went back to staring at his ceiling, smiling. "I knew it was real," he whispered, the last thought to go through his mind before sleep found him.

Terrible visions of war and death ravaged his sleep that night. In his dream, he could do nothing to help the people of Toratoga, and he eventually met his death while trying to defend them. The fall of the Goldwood Forest resulted from his death. The inhabitants of the forest became slaves to the horrible King Ro. He hated the dream and forced himself awake to escape it.

He didn't sleep anymore that night.

When he finally crawled out of bed just around eight in the morning, his mom made a comment about how awful he looked. He did look bad, and he felt worse. He thought that the dream he'd had during the night was real and would really happen to him. He thought he would die if he went with Alice. But he would go. His mother confirmed that Toratoga was real, and if there was no other hope but him, then he would go.

He didn't eat much of his breakfast, and when his mom left for work, he barely made an effort to say anything to her.

"Remember not to go up to the Hanson house today, Jacob," she said on her way out the door.

27

"I know, Mom," he replied, still staring at his bowl of cereal. His little bits of Frosted Flakes were fighting a losing battle against the milk.

"Love ya, Jacob, I'll see you after work."

"'Bye."

Jacob always did what his mom said; if she gave a straight demand to not do something, he didn't do it. He was respectful of her wishes, and in turn, she was respectful of him. Until that day, and the day when he'd first visited the house, he always did what his mom asked of him with no questions.

That day, Jacob went to the Hanson house at the end of Ash Street. As he walked toward the house, and what he thought, his doom, he looked back at his house only once. "Today, I will be brave," he whispered as he gazed upon the yellow house one last time.

He walked down that road with the speed of a man facing execution, but only because he thought he was. He walked with his head up, showing his pride to do something great before he died. "At least I'll try."

At last, he reached the house without any day dreams of sinking into the grass of the front lawn. He went around back where he thought Alice would be waiting for him, probably up in a tree. To his surprise, she wasn't anywhere in the backyard. He wandered up to the back door of the house, expecting it to be locked like the front door the day before, but it wasn't.

The back door opened to a darkness that even the sun seemed afraid to penetrate. Jacob stepped into a hallway. Two doors led off the hall. The first was a laundry room that had windows facing the outside to let in the sunlight. The second was a bathroom. Its window was covered by the overgrown hedges outside.

Jacob wandered down the hall and through the kitchen, a large rack of pots and pans still hung above the island with the stove and dishwasher. The kitchen was larger than any he'd ever seen, once again reminding him of a castle. He crossed to the opposite side of the kitchen where the door led into the dining room. Four chairs sat around a long table.

Finally, he found the staircase beside the living room. He guessed that after seeing Alice in the attic that that was where the portal would be. He climbed the stairs right past the second floor and on into the attic.

The attic was a large room with several boxes covered in sheets. Matching windows on each side of the room were the only sources of light. Standing in the center of the room was a large bathtub, an old fashioned one with claw feet. But this one was completely black. Jacob suddenly remembered what his mom had said about Mr. Hanson collecting antiques.

Jacob stared at the tub. Despite the fact that there was no faucet, the tub was filled to the brim with water, which was clear and very still and reflected everything in the room."

"This has to be it." The bathtub was so out of place in the attic that if felt eerie to be near it.

Of course this is it. There's nothing else that could be it.

"Shut up, Taylor," Jacob replied, and all at once, Taylor did shut up. Jacob realized that he didn't need him anymore. He had a quest before him, and he had to concentrate on it, not the absence of his brother. And soon, he wouldn't be alone anymore.

Then he noticed a small piece of paper lying right next to the tub. Jacob took the paper and unfolded it. He smiled when he saw it was from Alice.

Jacob,

Too much time has already passed since I first left Toratoga. I had to get back, but I have the assurance of your promise that you will come. All you need to do to get through the portal is climb into the basin of water and lie down. Once there, simply pull the plug and let the water take you to Toratoga.

Waiting through the portal,

Alice

Jacob stared at the note for a full minute before deciding to go through with it. He walked over to the tub and looked at himself in the water's still surface. He could've sworn he saw trees next to his reflection, but it must have been his imagination.

He put his hands on the edge of the tub and put one leg, shoe and all, into the water. The cold water sent chills through his flesh. Despite the shivers, he pulled his other leg into the water. He was shocked to see that even though he'd climbed into the water, none of it spilled over the top. It was right up to the edge, but the water stayed still.

He sat in the water and, taking one final breath of air, submerged himself under its surface. He reached the chain that held the plug and tugged at it. With some effort, it finally came free. He could feel the water begin to drain.

The water tugged at him, pulling him along with it. He reached up to the edge of the tub to hold on, but he stopped at the sight of his hand. He could see through it, and as he watched, it stretched out to join the water going down the drain. He became a part of the water, so he could flow. His body stretched out like the rubber bands he and Taylor used to shoot at each other. Fear rushed through him. He had no idea what was happening, but he hoped he would make it out.

Chapter 4

The Other World

Jacob almost gave up living to see twelve. He needed air. He opened his eyes and saw that he was just inches from the surface of water. He kicked with his legs and gasped gratefully as the air once more flowed through his body after his face emerged from the water. Tears streamed from his eyes. He never wanted to do that again.

He was in a lake. Everything was dark, but somehow, he was able to see beyond even the shores of the lake. It was as if the Sun's rays were shining grey light instead of yellow. He stared around, taking in everything. He saw trees in the distance that reminded him of the scary shadows he had to fight to get out of bed in the middle of the night for a drink of water. Their limbs were leafless and scratched at the sky as the wind blew them. And they were the biggest trees he'd ever seen.

The lake itself was miles across, but he found himself floating very close to the southern shore. He wasted no time in swimming for it.

Once on shore, he looked up at the sky through the clearing over the lake, and he was surprised to see a tinge of blue to the sky. "Color," he thought. Then he remembered what Alice told him about the Grebbles remaining blue.

Everything lacked any amount of joy, and all the colors were oddly missing, leaving only grays and blacks and browns. He looked at his hands and saw only gray through the colorless fog Alice told him about.

As far as he could see, there were great trees, some over forty feet in diameter. "This has to be Toratoga," he said without realizing he spoke. A puff of fog escaped his mouth with his words, but he didn't notice the cold. He concentrated on the reality of his situation. His wet clothes dripped all around him, wetting the black soil at his feet.

He'd found the world he was supposed to save, but now looking at all the devastation, he didn't know how he'd ever be able to do it. Even the hope inside Jacob that convinced him to get into that bathtub was snuffed out in this world.

Bits of gray sand fell on him and stuck to his damp clothes and hair. The sand came from the trees. They were slowly falling apart, becoming sand. Jacob turned to get away from the sight because it saddened him.

He walked to the nearest tree. The rough bark looked like any tree in his world, only it was black and gray. The few leaves on the tree were all brown, although they looked fully alive. He craned his neck back to try to see to the top, but found it was impossible.

Jacob had indeed found the Goldwood Forest in Toratoga, just as Alice told him he would. But Alice wasn't waiting for him. She wasn't where she said she would be, nor were any other life forms. No birds or snakes or monkeys. The forest around him was completely silent.

He walked away from the lake. Once again, he found himself feeling the ring in his pocket for some sort of assurance, some sort of pleasant memory to get him through the heaviness of this world.

He walked, continuously looking up at the trees that towered over him like he was walking down a sidewalk in Manhattan. Each tree had the same features of black and grey bark with brown leaves. Being in the unfamiliar land, he found that everything looked the same.

He trudged on through the forest.

Eventually, he came to a small creek. He knelt beside it and scooped some of the water out with his hand and lifted it to his face. He drank deeply from the water and almost spit it back out. The water had a strange coppery taste to it, as if the water wasn't just water, but very diluted blood.

He crossed the creek, wanting to forget the taste of that water, and continued on through the forest. Everything had an eerie heavy feeling like he was walking with a blanket draped over him.

He walked on and on for nearly four hours before he noticed the trees beginning to thin out. He looked up more and more often, noticing how much more of the sky he could see. He stopped to rest frequently, wondering why he'd come. He began to get hungry as the morning gave way to afternoon.

Fine gray sand began to cover the ground as he walked, and the air became colder and stung his skin as the wind blew. As the trees thinned out, great dunes of gray sand rose up around him, and the wind blew harder. He shivered, but continued to walk.

He trudged on for another hour before he realized he'd left the trees behind almost entirely. There were a few remnants of the trees scattered about the land, but as far as Jacob could see, he'd walked out of the forest. The wind blew hard outside of the wood, and the temperature seemed to drop ten degrees every minute, at least to Jacob it did who'd gone and left his jacket at home.

He pulled his arms inside his t-shirt and crossed them over his chest to warm himself, but he didn't turn around. His mind was not clear, so he didn't realize that he'd walked the wrong way. And so, Jacob went on walking to the south in hopes of finding Alice or some of her people. "At least," he thought, "maybe I can find some place warm."

The land stretched out before him, and the Sun slowly descended into its bed for the evening. Jacob began to worry greatly about what was going to happen to him in this strange world. He'd only camped out a time or two and even those times were in a tent in his own front yard with his brother. The thought of those happier times made tears come to his eyes.

You shouldn't cry. That's not very tough, Make-Believe-Taylor said.

"I thought I told you to go away," Jacob responded.

Yes, well, you're alone now, aren't you?

Jacob nodded and continued to walk. In truth, he welcomed his brother's voice just as much as he would have welcomed a fireplace and warm bed.

"Do you think it was a mistake coming here?"

No. Look at the adventures we're having.

"Yeah, loads of fun."

Just live through this and you can make it back home to write your book.

"Taylor, I don't even know how to get back home."

Sure, you just...well, I don't rightly know either.

Jacob's hope diminished until he saw two trees ahead of him. These trees were smaller than those of the Goldwood Forest, but they looked like they might provide some shelter. He ran for them. He sat with his back leaning on the bough of one. His body shivered.

"Taylor, I'm so cold," he said.

I suppose I would be too, if I were actually there.

"Should I just sleep here tonight?"

What else can you do?

Jacob did feel very tired and his legs ached from all the walking. He began to close his eyes when someone yelled at him.

"Hey, you there, who're you talkin' to?" the voice said.

Jacob jumped to his feet and looked around him. He'd been too tired and too cold to notice that right next to the trees, a black road cut through the sand. He heard someone coming up the road, although he could see no one, his eyes not quite adjusting to the moonlight. Before he could decide what to do, the voice's owner was next to him, grabbing hold of his shoulder. Jacob cried out in surprise.

"Who're you?" the voice asked again, and as Jacob watched, a bearded face came out of the darkness to look him in the eye. He had a helm above his brow, and Jacob noted quickly just how strong the soldier's grip on his shoulder was.

"I'm...my name is Jacob," he managed to spill out in spite of his fear.

"A lil' boy out here on 'is own? What're 'ou wearin'?"

Jacob looked down at himself and realized quite suddenly just how strange he must look in his jeans and t-shirt. "Uh, they're just clothes, sir," he finally said. Despite his fear, he remembered the manners his mother so urgently taught him.

"Well, they're nothin' like I've e'er seen before. A'right, watcha doin' out here anyway?"

"I, uh, I just got lost. I couldn't find my way back home."

"Where're you from? Not from around here, I s'pect."

"No, I come from Cottageville," Jacob said, forgetting momentarily that he and his mother moved to Abbey. His lapse of memory worked in his favor for Cottageville is a small seaport village in the southwest part of the kingdom of Toratoga.

"Long way from Cottageville, aren't we?"

"Well, yes." Surprise washed over Jacob as the words struck him. "They know about Cottageville?" he thought.

"Well, I can' leave you out here ta freeze ta death. I'm jus' finishin' my rounds, I'll take ya to my house where my wife will take care of ya. She always says I don't bring home enough guests." He laughed heartily at himself.

Jacob, too stunned to believe his good fortune, nodded his agreement.

"Right, name's William, by the way. And you're Jacob. Say, you aren' missin' a finger are ya?"

Fear washed over Jacob all over again and continued to cascade down onto him as William began to laugh. "I'm only kiddin' ya," William said between laughs. Then seeing the look on Jacob's face he said, "You've heard of Jacob Nine-fingers, haven't ya?"

Jacob, unsure of how to answer, nodded slowly.

"Sure, everyone's heard o' the one with nine fingers who's going to overthrow the kingdom." He began laughing again. When he finally stopped his joyous belly jiggling, he helped Jacob onto his black horse, and he walked beside it. He wrapped Jacob in a saddle blanket that smelled like sweat, but Jacob welcomed the warmth it provided. Jacob could not believe that everyone knew about the Prophecy. He'd thought that only the Orns knew.

He led them down the road to a large stone wall with a wide wooden gate in it.

"Dang Orns," William said. "Ne'er had a gate 'fore this damn war broke out. They decide the king's too evil or somethin' and attack. We had to build this wall or we'd've been taken by the Orns long ago."

He knocked three times on the heavy gate.

"Do you know the password?" a small raspy voice shouted over the wall.

"Ham, shut ya mouth, it's jus' me William."

The latches on the gate clanked open, and before him, Jacob saw a small town unfolding on either side of the road. The buildings, which were houses and shops, were wooden structures covered in mud for insulation. Most were very small, but a few were quite larger. Several small lamps lit the road, so Jacob could see people wandering in and out of them.

As William led the horse into town, the houses and shops passed under Jacob's gaze. One immediately caught his attention. Lots of loud talking, laughing, glass clanging together, and singing all radiated from inside the building. And he realized with awe and wonder that he was looking at a tavern. A real tavern, just like the ones in the stories about knights and legends of old.

William stopped the horse in front of a small cottage just off the main road. He helped Jacob down off the horse and said, "Wait here, I'll put the horse in the stable, and we'll go in together." Jacob nodded and gave the saddle blanket back. He stood outside the door with his arms still in his shirt to retain the warmth from the blanket. He watched random people walk down the main road of the town. Most were soldiers dressed in the same fashion as William, and all were men.

"All righ', let's go," William said as soon as he returned. He turned away from the road and saw William already opening the door to his humble home. Gray firelight spilled out onto the street along with the warmth that came with it.

A small wooden table sat directly in front of a fireplace in the center of the room. A thin woman with dark hair and clothes that looked as if they hadn't been cleaned for quite sometime sat at one end of the table. Two little boys sat in front of the fire facing the door, fidgeting and waiting for their food. Above the fireplace was a loft that was accessible by a wooden ladder.

"'Ello, family," William said as he walked in. His wife smiled brightly at him, and the boys jumped from their seats to run to him, but all motion stopped as Jacob walked into the room. As the heat washed over him, he pulled his arms from his shirt. They looked at him with curiosity. His clothes and hair were so different from their own, and he looked much cleaner than any of the others did.

William watched his family's response to the newcomer. "This is Jacob," he finally said. "I found 'im out on the road half froze ta death. Thought he could stay here for the evenin'."

His wife stood to greet Jacob. "Welcome to our home, Jacob. My name is Lorrie, and these are our two boys, Harold and Francis." The boys stared at Jacob with wonder; they were slightly younger than he. "We're just sitting down to eat," Lorrie continued. "Are you hungry?"

"Yes, ma'am," Jacob responded.

They sat around the table that night, Jacob feeling right at home for the first time since his own family split. Harold and Francis acted the same way he and Taylor used to act he noticed with a slight pang of sadness. But the night was good. Lorrie gave Jacob some clothes to wear so he wouldn't look so out of place in their small village. None of William's family had ever ventured as far over as Cottageville, so they assumed Jacob's dress was common on the seaport.

Lorrie made a bed for Jacob in the loft with Harold and Francis, and after the boys climbed the ladder for their sleep that evening, Lorrie set about cleaning the house while William smoked his pipe. Finally Lorrie sat with William after she was sure the boys were sleeping.

"Did you see, Willy?" she asked him.

"Yeah, I saw," he responded quietly. "I didn't want ta believe it, but you can't deny it, no matter how much you try not ta believe."

"But he's just a little boy, no different than Frank or Harry."

"I know it, but that don't change the king's law. He's ta be reported."

"Isn't there any way we could let him go?"

"Lorrie, listen ta yourself, your talkin' abou' treason. We get caught, we're dead."

"I know. You're right. What are you going to do?"

"I'll take 'im ta the castle tomorrow. King Ro can have 'im. I don't want the little boy's death on my hands any more 'an you do, but we've got no choice."

"Oh, William, do you really think it's him, the one who's come to take back the kingdom?"

"How many other Jacobs have you seen walking around missing an index finger?"

"You're right, William, you always are. I love you."

"And I love you."

Lorrie went to bed, but William continued to sit at the table staring into the dying firelight. Jacob had been very careful at first to hide his hand from William's family, but the more comfortable he got, the more he forgot about its importance. William noticed it first, then Lorrie. The boys were having too much fun with their new guest that they never noticed his missing finger. Jacob slept in the hay next to Harold and Francis without a care in the world while William tried to figure out how to take Jacob to the castle without him noticing. After a while, he decided he'd just have to take him, and when the dawn broke the surface of the night sky, Jacob found himself riding on the horse with William, wearing his new, warmer clothes, but feeling a cold dread in his heart nonetheless.

He was going to see King Ro.

Chapter 5

King Ro

Jacob sat in front of William on the saddle watching the land of Toratoga flow slowly by him. At first, he had no idea where William wanted to take him so early in the morning, but the truth dawned on him as gradually as the sun working its way up in the sky. A huge black castle sat on the distant horizon, and Jacob felt horrible assurance of who lived in that castle.

A steady breeze blew out over the land and eventually they left behind all traces of trees and the gray sand, as the black grass grew thickly up through the soil.

William rode quietly behind Jacob, feeling guilt weigh down his gut like a ball of lead. He no more wanted to take Jacob to King Ro than Jacob wanted to go, but he knew he and his family would die horrible deaths if the king found out. And he would find out. He always did. And he should know after his neighbor Raleigh was taken by the King's Grebbles a month back and never seen again. The people of his village lived in that constant fear of King Ro. Everyone did.

"Why are you a soldier?" Jacob suddenly asked amid the steady clopping of the horse's hooves. His breath came out in a little puff of fog, but he didn't feel the cold; he only felt the fear of what lie ahead.

"I joined the Guard when I was eighteen during the time of peace," William said, reflecting on happier times in his mind. "Everyone my age did, almos', and we were able ta make a livin' just by patrollin' our area and keepin' our families and neighbors safe. Although there was nothin' ta keep 'em safe from.

"Then things went bad. The Orns began attackin' random villages in hopes to overthrow the king. That's when the king brought the Grebbles back from the East. By that point, it was simply too late to drop out of the Guard without endangerin' my family. I do my duty for my safety."

Jacob fell back into his silence, thinking about what William told him.

As they neared the castle, Jacob tried talking to William about where they were going, but he refused to say anything about it. As the city at the foot of the castle came into view, Jacob's fear became too much for him to withstand, and reluctantly, William finally told him the truth.

"I have ta take ya ta the king, Jacob. I'm sorry, but if I don', my family will be in danger. We've reached terrible days in Toratoga, and I don' quite understand it."

Jacob's mind nearly collapsed with the pressure of William's reasoning. He realized that in order to keep the soldier's family safe, he would have to enter the black castle. After that, he didn't know what would happen to him, but he hoped that William would at least be safe. He suddenly felt very brave.

"Do you still support the king?" Jacob asked.

"I haven' really thought abou' it. But why shouldn' I? There is no other altern'tive, is there? Not like I could join the Orns."

"But why not? The Orns would protect you."

He guffawed. "Protect me? Half the time they're tryin' to kill me."

"They're only trying to protect their lands. Besides, doesn't the king try to kill you?"

"Not once 'as the king attempted any foul behavior toward me."

"Then why are you taking me to him?"

"All righ', I know what you're tryin' ta do, but I don' have a choice. I'm sorry."

They rode on in silence, Jacob's words weaving a complex set of thoughts through William's mind.

At long last, after the sun began its descent in the sky, they reached the city gate. The gate opened after William announced his purpose, and the horse led them into the city.

Jacob was amazed to see the beauty of the city that fell before him. Even without its color, he could see the architectural ingeniousness. Most of the buildings, which were houses, hotels, theaters, and barracks for soldiers, were carved from stone. The city was built on a hill that ended in a great black castle. Jacob's eyes were wide, taking in as much as he possibly could.

About an hour after entering the city, they reached the outer wall of the castle. This wall made the one around William's village look like a joke. It towered over the two travelers by twenty feet. Guards clad in black armor stood at attention in front of the gate. As soon as William rode up on his horse, their spears were out and pointing at him.

"What business have you at the castle?" the one on the left asked.

"I've brought the nine-fingered Jacob ta 'is gates," William said.

At once, the guard on the left stepped forward to examine Jacob. The guard on the right produced a black bag after the former guard confirmed his missing finger. The bag came down over Jacob's head, and he was knocked unconscious. Although Jacob didn't know it, William himself was almost knocked out after he protested their treatment of Jacob, but at the threat of imprisonment, he gave up and let them take the boy. He stayed that night at the barracks in town and early the next morning he went back home to his wife and children where his mind never fully recovered from his meeting with Jacob.

Meanwhile, the soldiers carried the limp body of the child through the outer gate, through the inner gate, and into the castle. They left him in a long gray room with a few torches lining the walls, sitting him in one of two chairs in the middle of the room facing each other. King Ro already sat in the opposite chair, waiting for Jacob. The soldiers woke Jacob with smelling salts.

"Hello, Jacob," King Ro said.

"Who's there?" he asked. He opened his eyes but could see nothing. They'd left the black bag on his head, which was throbbing from the blow they'd given him.

"Don't you know?" The fog cleared from Jacob's mind, although his head ached horribly, he remembered where William took him.

"Are you King Ro?" Jacob asked.

"Yes."

"What do you want from me?"

"I want you to see your king while you are in Toratoga."

He pulled the bag from Jacob's head. Jacob blinked, allowing his eyes to adjust from the sudden brightness. Standing in front of him was a tall man in a white robe that reached all the way to floor. The hood was pulled up, concealing his face in shadow. His hands were inside his sleeves in front of him. Jacob could see no flesh, only the white robe and the shadows cast from the gray light.

"I am King Ro."

Jacob watched as King Ro's hands rose out of the cloth of his robe to the sides of his hood. Thin white fingers protruded from large boney. The long pointed fingernails of his pinkies sliced through the air like sharp blades. Black vine tattoos covered the flesh along the bottom of his hands and along his forearms as far as the cloth allowed him to see.

King Ro lowered his hood, revealing his face. Long white hair flowed out of the robe and down his back to rest between his shoulders. His eyes were entirely black, and above them were wild white eyebrows that looked like two branches off a dead tree. His lips parted in a smile showing off his straight white teeth. Jacob noticed that one of his nostrils had a white powder around it. The black vine tattoo continued up the side of his neck, stopping halfway up. He was easily the scariest human being Jacob could ever remember seeing in his thirteen years. Jacob only wanted to cry, to crawl into his mother's lap and let her rock him in her chair.

"Jacob, welcome to the Court of King Ro. I am delighted that you could make it. I am even more delighted to see that you are just a child," the king said, that smile never leaving his face. He saw the boy's fear and rejoiced in it. His voice was deep and booming in the long room.

"I am your king while you are here in Toratoga. Certain races of my land have deemed me evil, and Jacob, I will deal with them. I have powers that cannot be matched by any in this land, and I will rule no matter what trickery the Orns and Elves try to pull on me.

"Nothing, Jacob, nothing you've heard about Toratoga, my great kingdom, is true." He broke off his speech and began to laugh, but his eyes never left Jacob's. "I can show you secrets of this world. But I won't unless you will show your devotion to me."

King Ro began to walk toward Jacob, bearing that same eerie smile. Jacob became mesmerized by the king's words, and he found he couldn't take his eyes off the king's. The black of his eyes almost seemed to swirl with color.

"I have been a good king, one of the best this land has ever seen. My men agree. I was able to reestablish contact and peace between humans and the Grebbles. I have brought Toratoga to a new era, an era where colors can be used as currency.

"And how do the people repay my kindnesses? They revolt against me. They force me and my kind into war, destroying much of the precious artifacts of Toratoga. Destroying so much of their own trees, their own homes, Jacob.

"You see, I am the king, and I am a good king. It's those forest dwellers that are *evil*. They rise up against their master and are continually ungrateful for me and my mercies. I am merciful no longer. Soon, I will unleash all of my powers on the Goldwood Forest. The Orns and Elves will remember their king." His voice, no longer booming and deep, grew with each word, rising higher and higher in pitch with his hysterics.

Finally, he regained his composure and said, "Jacob, I want to show you something."

The king, now standing beside Jacob's chair, held out his hand for him. Jacob saw that the lines in the king's palm were also decorated with black ink. He looked from the king's hand to his face and, hesitating only for a moment, placed his own hand in the king's.

The king led him around the chair to the front of the room behind Jacob's chair. A large table sat against the wall. Jacob was shocked to see that the table was a deep red. Four candles sat on the table casting gray light over a bowl sitting in the center. The king walked with Jacob up to the table. The bowl was full of a powdery substance, something like ash.

"This has opened my eyes, Jacob. This powder, this ash, keeps my eyes open and full of life. You can share in this with me, prove to those Orns and Elves that I am good, and maybe you can stop us from going to war. I mean that is why you are here, isn't it?"

King Ro dipped his right pinky fingernail into the powder and raised a large amount of it up to his nostril. He breathed deeply into the powder until all of it was gone. Jacob watched King Ro's eyes change from black to a bright green that glowed in the gray candlelight.

"Ah..." he said, relishing in the feeling the powder gave him. "Now you, Jacob." The king looked at Jacob, eyes full of greed and hunger. The green of the king's eyes slowly faded back to black.

Jacob looked at the powder. "What is it?" he asked.

"You will find out as soon as you've tried it," the king replied.

Jacob raised his right hand to the dish and pinched a small portion of it between his middle finger and his thumb. He raised it to his face, but before he put it in his nose, he looked at the king for reassurance. The king had completely overwhelmed Jacob's thought processes, but as he looked at the king, he saw the black vine tattoo on his neck crawl like the severed leg of a crushed spider up the rest of his neck before stopping at his jaw line.

It grew. Make-Believe-Taylor whispered to him. Jacob was shocked to know that he was still there.

Watching the tattoo crawl up the king's neck broke the spell over Jacob, and he once again regained control of his own thoughts. He looked back at the powder and made a quick decision.

He lifted his fingers to his nostril, and while the king was watching, he pretended to inhale it. He coughed and lifted his left hand to block the coughing while his right hand put the powder in the pocket of his tunic. He continued the coughing, in hopes of distracting the king. The king began laughing madly, and Jacob knew he believed.

"Now, Jacob, don't you feel better?"

Jacob nodded, careful not to look into the king's eyes.

"Come this way. Now I can show you some of the true wonders of Toratoga."

King Ro led Jacob to the right of the table. They walked right up to the wall and stood before it. The king reached inside his white robe and pulled from it a small vile containing black liquid. He pulled the cork from it and poured two drops onto a small grey brick in front of the wall. The brick turned bright red for an instant, and in that instant, the wall vanished to reveal a small gray chamber.

On the far side of the chamber was a large fireplace with a huge fire burning bright gray light all over the room. The rest of the room was dark and full of dancing shadows as the flames jumped from log to log in the fireplace. The only thing Jacob could make out in the strange light was a slumped figure sitting on a chair in the center of the room. He followed King Ro into the chamber, the king's boot steps resounding off the walls like the echoes of Jacob's heartbeats inside his chest.

As they neared the slumped figure, he was able to tell that it was a female. She was bound around the legs with a thin silvery rope and her arms were bound around her back in the same way. A large black bowl rested on the floor beside her. She raised her eyes to look at King Ro and his new guest as they walked toward her, and Jacob saw no fear in her eyes, only a proud determination.

Once beside the slumped woman, Jacob realized that she was an Orn. His hands began to shake slightly. "What do you think of the king's secret chamber?" King Ro asked the Orn. She simply stared up at him in response. "All right, not going to talk? That's fine. I don't need you to talk anyway." King Ro produced a slender knife with a curved blade. It was sharp and shimmered in the firelight.

"There is so much power in the eyes," he said.

The knife point slid easily through the girl's right eyelid. She let out no scream as King Ro cut out her gray eye from its socket. Her blood was black as it crept down her cheeks to her chin. Jacob stood horrified, watching helplessly as the eye fell into the king's hand.

"Jacob, come here," King Ro said to him. Something sick squirmed inside of him, but he stood next to him and tried not to look at the bleeding Orn, her one good eye still staring out at them.

"These are burned for my powder. The rest is discarded, thrown out into the sea south of here. I don't like to keep bodies lying around my castle. It lowers the morale." He laughed in a shrill high cackle.

Jacob watched as King Ro bent over the bowl and dropped the eye into it. Flames burst to life on it almost instantly, and soon all that was left was a small pile of ash.

"Now, Jacob," the king continued. "Take her other eye." The knife handle was warm in Jacob's hand from the king's own flesh. Fear really began to grip him once more. He originally thought that he came to the castle to die, but instead, he faced a nightmare.

Then the Orn spoke.

"Thank you, O King, for delivering me from this world," the Orn said, her grey eye searching over the king's face. "Your lies, your treachery, your horrid evil will be dealt with. Soon, Jacob Nine-fingers will be here to deal with you. You will be destroyed along with your wickedness."

Jacob, his heart dropping for a moment, considered attacking the king right then. The king's laughter broke him from the thought.

"You silly girl, Jacob Nine-fingers is right here with me. He is helping me kill you."

"You lie!" she screamed. Her shrill scream echoed through the chamber and through Jacob's head. But while she screamed, her eye flew to Jacob and down his body to his right hand that clutched the knife that was still dripping her black blood. She saw his missing finger and knew it was him.

For Jacob, the whole reason he came to this world was suddenly presented before him. Maybe he wouldn't be able to help the entire Orn civilization, but, he thought, at least he could help this one. Fear and determination fought a bitter battle inside of him in that moment. He closed his eyes briefly, and squeezed the knife in his hands. In that instant, everything went quiet; every noise, every movement, fell away.

Jacob opened his eyes.

He gasped as he gazed about the room. The firelight, no longer grey, cast its bright yellow light around a gorgeous white room. The king and Orn found their full colors, including the red blood on the Orn's cheek, but neither moved. Jacob stared between the two trying to understand how everything suddenly regained its original color, but lost its movement.

The knife handle began to burn hot in his hand. The handle was gold and ornate, and the blade shone beautiful silver in the firelight with little drops of red blood falling away from it. He looked at it as if seeing it for the first time, not letting go of it despite the heat. He drew magic from the handle that some former magician had stored there. Jacob, of course, had no idea.

Not questioning his luck, he ran around the Orn and cut the ropes from her arms and legs. When he finished, he looked at the king. His white robes and hair were now jet black with streaks of red. He looked like a nightmare to that thirteen year-old boy, like something that crawled from the shadows surrounding his bed at night. Jacob was more afraid of this King Ro than the one he'd been with all evening. "This is the real king," Jacob thought. "I am seeing everything how it should be."

He stood studying the eyes of King Ro when the king blinked. Fear shot through him, and he lost his hold on the moment. Everything came rushing back to the way it was when he first entered Toratoga. He stood facing the king, and King Ro tilted his head, curiously examining him. Jacob hadn't moved back to his place next to the king. He'd moved several feet without anyone seeing him move.

"What have you done, boy?" the king asked in a quiet voice. Jacob couldn't shake the nightmare version of the king he'd just seen.

Before Jacob could answer, however, the Orn, realizing she was free, leapt to her feet and dove into the king. Taken by surprise, his body went limp with the impact. The Orn threw the king into the wall where he crumpled to the floor.

Jacob, wasting no time, grabbed the Orn by the hand and ran to the opposite side of the room that he had entered. There was a small wooden door in the stone grey wall. Jacob opened it and led the Orn through. He still held the knife, so he stuffed it in the pocket of his tunic with the powder.

"I knew you'd save me," the Orn said, looking at Jacob with her one eye.

"No time for that now, we have to find a way out of here," Jacob replied. They found themselves standing in a long room with a huge table.

The table itself looked like a football game could be played on it. The hall was decorated with various tapestries that were all robbed of their colors, and on one wall, a large stone fireplace sat.

"There are no other doors in this room."

"What should we do?" the Orn asked.

"Maybe there is a secret passageway in the fireplace."

"A secret passageway? How could you know that?"

"There are passageways in castles all the time in movies. This can't be that different." Jacob ran to that fireplace in hopes of finding a way out.

He looked all over the stones and found that nothing seemed out of place. He tried pulling the candelabras that hung on each side of the mantle but neither gave. He felt that he was running out of time and was ready to give up on a secret passage when the Orn discovered it for him.

One single drop of black blood crawled down the Orn's cheek like the final tear of a hard cry. The blood dropped off the chin of the Orn and landed on a smooth grey brick in front of the fireplace. Instantly, the blood soaked into the brick, turning it a bright red, but only for a moment. As soon as the color went back to grey, the back of the fireplace opened up on a steep, spiraling staircase.

"I forgot about the king doing that," Jacob said.

"What was it?" the Orn asked.

"Your blood landed on that brick and opened the door. He keeps a vile of Orn blood with him to open these doors."

They climbed down the staircase as quickly as they could without being a danger to themselves. The dark stairway spiraled down to the main floor of the castle.

Above them, they heard King Ro scream.

"They'll be after us now," Jacob said, and they made their way down the stairs a little faster.

At the bottom of the stairs they found a large door. Jacob reached to open the door, and from above, they heard footsteps echoing down the stairs. The king screamed for the soldiers to find the Orn and Jacob.

"They better not escape the castle," King Ro shouted from above.

Jacob pushed the door open, and he and the Orn fell into a hall. The door shut behind them, concealed behind a large painting of a very beautiful woman. Jacob looked around and decided, on a whim, to run to the right. They passed more paintings, some strange weaponry, and one very large suit of armor. Finally, they reached the top of a staircase that led down to the entryway of the castle. Jacob breathed a sigh of relief.

The crashing of heavy footfalls sounded off the high ceilings of the hallway and warned the fugitives of the coming guards. He barely managed to keep his balance as he descended the stairs to the massive wooden doors, tugging the Orn down the stairs after him. Once on the floor, Jacob slammed himself into the door.

The footfalls came ever closer to the two, but Jacob found his strength lacking when it came to opening the door. He pushed, but it wouldn't budge. "Come on, just open," Jacob pleaded with the door. The Orn then stepped up beside him and pushed on the door. He watched the veins in her arms pop out and gaped as the door swung slowly open, revealing the courtyard of the castle.

Jacob and the Orn stepped out into the night air just as the guards reached the top of the stairs.

Chapter 6

Jacob's Flight

Jacob and the Orn darted through the courtyard of the castle grounds. A few torches scattered here and there revealed a few of the king's Guard resting on their night patrol. The pair ran for the gates of the inner walls. The king, leading his Guard, exploded out of the castle. The Guards on night patrol were at once on their feet, looking at the king in surprise.

"GET THEM!" King Ro screamed at the soldiers.

The soldiers wasted no time chasing after the two. Jacob and the Orn picked up their pace, but the soldiers were very fast. As they neared the gate, Jacob could see that the soldiers were opening it. He nearly stopped running when he saw why they opened the gate. Two large creatures were walking in through the gate. Their white hair was blowing behind them in the breeze and their blue flesh glowing in the grey moonlight. Jacob realized he was seeing Grebbles for the first time.

The soldiers running behind Jacob stopped as the Grebbles came in through the gate. The king came up behind them and began to laugh. "You are caught now, Jacob Nine-fingers," the king said.

But the fugitives didn't stop running. The sweet smell of candy and flowers entered Jacob's nostrils as he neared the Grebbles. The blue creatures looked curiously at the pair running toward them, the gate slowly closing in the background. Jacob and the Orn were able to run right between the Grebbles before the king screamed at them, "Grab them, you fools!"

They slipped through the closing gate before the Grebbles reacted, and the soldiers at the gate slammed it closed before the king could tell them to stop. The guards on the outside of the gate tried to stop Jacob and the Orn from escaping, but their encompassing armor slowed them amazingly.

Jacob and the Orn gained a good lead on the king's guards and managed to weave their way through the town without many people noticing them. By the time the gate was opened and the guards back on the trail, no one really knew where the two had gone.

They managed to sneak down a trashed-out alley between two of the stone structures that most likely served as houses. Jacob crawled along the garbage with the Orn following closely behind him. They picked their way through the secluded alleyway without any prying eyes watching them. When they emerged, they found themselves on the edge of town, right next to the wall.

"Do you think we're safe?" Jacob asked the Orn, panting slightly.

"I think this may be close to the spot where they captured me. I was sent to spy on the town and, if by chance, the king. I think I got more than I bargained for," the Orn said.

"I'm Jacob by the way."

"My name is Aural."

"How far do you think it is to your home?"

"Well, it's close to two days to the forest from here."

"How will we survive with the king after us?"

"There are some hiding places along the way. We shouldn't risk open fire to give away our location."

"Okay, how do we get over this wall?"

"We don't go over it, we go through it. There's a hole in the wall close to here."

She turned to her right and, at the base of the wall, saw what she needed. A small shrub plant sat at the bottom of a fissure in the wall. Aural led Jacob to the shrub and pulled it aside to reveal a small hole, just large enough for them to fit through.

"Cool," Jacob said as he bent to look through the hole. He could see the land stretching out beyond it. A few scattered trees promised some hiding places to the fugitives.

"Okay, I'll go first," Aural said. "Run straight to that patch of trees, Jacob, and we'll meet there to decide what to do."

Jacob nodded his concurrence, and Aural ducked through the hole. Holding the shrub aside, he watched as she ran to the trees. He began to crawl through the hole when he heard soldiers yelling and running somewhere behind him. Then the lunatic voice of the king broke over him.

"The first one who finds them gets to eat with their family tonight," the king shouted. "But if they escape..."

Jacob crawled through, ignoring the rest of what King Ro said. He turned back to make sure the shrub was in place then ran for the trees. Aural hunched down beside the bough of one large tree, waiting for him.

"We have to hurry, Jacob, it won't be long before they realize we've escaped."

They ran on through the rest of the night, constantly stopping amid bushes, trees, or just laying flat on the ground. They stood on a hill and looked back at the town and the black castle that loomed over it, always keeping watch. They managed to put a great amount of distance between themselves and the city. Shortly before sundown of the next day, they reached the grey sand.

Before they entered the sand wasteland, Aural paused to talk to her hero. "Jacob, what happened in the king's chamber?"

"What do you mean?"

"Well, I thought I was dead, and next thing I know, my ropes were cut and you were facing the king. So, what happened?"

"I don't know. He wanted me to remove your other eye, and I was so nervous I closed my eyes. When I opened them, everything was frozen and all the color returned. The knife began to burn in my hand, so I decided to cut away your ropes."

Her one eye grew wide. "I think I know what that means. But how do you think the king knew about the prophecy?"

"What?"

"I mean that the prophecy was made by an Orn and held secret by the Orns, but the king knew about you."

Jacob thought about that for a moment. "And William, too, knew about the prophecy. How could they know?"

"Who's William?"

60

"Aural, we have to run. They're coming!"

And so they were. Several soldiers and four Grebbles followed a great black stallion that put to shame any horse Jacob had ever seen. The stallion carried King Ro whose hair flew up around his crown giving him the look of a horned demon.

They ran. They ran for the hope of seeing another day. They ran as fast as their small legs could carry them.

Jacob's lungs pumped inside of his chest and a stitch worked around in his sides. But nothing could make him stop running. He couldn't tell if the king and his men saw him or not, but he knew that if he slowed at all, it wouldn't be long before they found him. He simply hoped that the night would conceal them until they could reach the forest.

The trees began to appear on the sand again.

They ran, even when the thundering hooves of the great beast could be heard behind them. A shout let them know that they'd been spotted. They kept their pace, but Jacob felt his legs giving up the fight, felt his lungs constricting against the pressure, and he knew he wouldn't last much longer. Then the Orn stopped him.

"Jacob, it's no use."

"What...do...you...mean?"

"We can't make it. They're right on our tail. I'll stay and fight. You go on to the forest."

"Are you crazy? I can't leave you behind."

"Jacob, you must. You are the one who can save us. Go. Just keep running. There is a small knot of trees not far from here, they've protected many of my people over the past few weeks, and they can conceal you now. One of my people will find you once you pass the edge of the forest."

"But..."

"Go, Jacob, the king is nearly here."

"Thank you, Aural."

"No, Jacob, thank you. Just save my world."

With that, Jacob turned and ran to the trees. He could hear behind him the jeers and shouts of victory when the king's men caught the Orn. He stopped when he finally reached the trees; he could just see their outline in the torches the soldiers carried. He saw three men surround Aural, but when they tried to grab her, she overpowered them. Her fists flew out wildly and connected severe blows to two of the men who went flying. The Grebbles, however, were stronger than she. Two of them grabbed her arms and held her tight.

"Is this how you save Toratoga, Jacob Nine-fingers?" King Ro mocked. He dismounted from the black beast and stared in Jacob's direction. "You tell the Orns that I am coming. No child will destroy my kingdom." King Ro pulled his sword from its sheath and drove it through Aural. Her body went limp and the Grebbles dropped it.

"Spread out," King Ro said to his soldiers and Grebbles. "Find the boy. I want him alive. Find him before he can reach the forest."

At the same moment the sword drove through Aural's body, all the trees near the king turned to grey sand and fell into a heaping pile. The wind caught bits of it and blew it around, adding it to the desert.

The king's soldiers split up and began to run around; the king himself turned back to the city, back to his castle. Jacob knew he should run, but he didn't want to leave Aural's body lying in the middle of the desert.

He started out of the trees toward the Orn, desperate in his grief, but before he could, a small blue light fell from the sky, followed by another, and then two more. They all landed in a circle around Aural's limp form. Once the lights landed, they took on a human form, and looked to Jacob like four women. They all bent around the body and, lifting the limp form, ascended back into the sky. Jacob started to cry but stopped himself; they were already gone from sight. He wondered if he'd even seen the blue ladies.

After watching the Orn he'd just rescued get murdered, Jacob turned to the north, back toward the forest, trying to understand the strange events he'd been through already.

To get to the forest, he would have to run fast and hope that no soldier saw him. Looking out at the tree line on the horizon, he thought he would be able to make it, and a small hope began to build in his chest. He ran.

As Jacob neared the forest line, his hope increased. He knew he would make it to the safety of the trees, and then would be welcomed into the Treetop City as a hero by the Orns.

He almost made it when a sweet smell entered his nostrils. The smell reminded him of walking down the street in Cottageville with his brother to the candy store where they would spend their hard earned allowance on some of the brightest and tastiest candy Jacob would ever remember.

He turned away from the forest and saw, to his heart's dismay, a large blue Grebble. The sweet candy smell was suddenly replaced by a repulsive smell that reminded him of the time he and Taylor were wandering through a field and found the half decomposed carcass of a deer.

The Grebble's breath was slow and steady, and its skin as bright as any blue Jacob had ever seen in the light of the rising Sun. Its white hair was drawn out from the top of its head in a great white ponytail. It was beautiful and yet the most frightening thing Jacob had ever seen, besides the true form of King Ro.

Knowing it was his only chance, Jacob turned and ran. He reached out his hand and just brushed a tree with his fingertips when the Grebble grabbed him, pulling him back from the safety of the trees. The Grebble held him up to his face and howled a screeching wail that echoed throughout the forest behind him. Jacob stared the thing right in the face. He no longer felt fear coursing through him but anger. He was angry for what they'd done to Aural. He was angry for how they'd treated him since he came to this world. He missed his mom, and he missed his bed. He wanted to go home, and this blue beast stood in his way.

"I'm supposed to take you back to the king. I'm supposed to take extra precautions with you, the nine fingered boy," the Grebble said in its beautifully terrible voice. "I don't see what the big deal is, though. I find it hard to believe that this little runt could escape the great King Ro and overthrow his kingdom. I think I may just bite your head off right now and be done with it."

"You are very near the edge of the forest," Jacob said, slowly reaching into his tunic to find the knife King Ro had given him. The Grebble stared at him. "Do you not feel fear?"

The Grebble laughed even harder at Jacob. "Why should I fear old gray wood?"

"It's not the wood you should fear, but the things inside of it. There are Orn Warriors inside of this wood, and they are far greater than you." Jacob had no idea what he was saying, but he could see the fear working its way through the Grebble.

"Orn Warriors?" he laughed. "No Grebble has fallen at the hand of an Orn for two-hundred years."

"Was that when they forced you from this land?"

The Grebble became furious at Jacob's remark and decided to rip out Jacob's throat with his teeth. He opened his mouth and pulled Jacob near, just near enough that Jacob could pull the king's knife from the pocket of his tunic and stab him with it. The blade sunk deep into the monster's shoulder. He pulled it back out, ready to stab again when the Grebble dropped him.

Jacob fell to the ground as the Grebble dropped him and let out a terrible scream. Blood poured out of its wounded shoulder. Jacob backed away from the monster, putting distance between them.

"You foolish boy." The Grebble stared at Jacob in fury, trying not to show the pain that coursed through its shoulder. Jacob held the knife, ready for the coming attack of the Grebble. When the monster came, he felt no fear, only a determination to see this to the end.

Arrows shot through the air around Jacob and impaled the Grebble. It fell forward, carried by its momentum, at Jacob's feet. He stared down at the dead Grebble in curious wonderment. Ten seconds later, he was surrounded by five Orn Warriors.

Chapter 7

The Orn Tribesmen

Jacob stood in the midst of the five Orns. They surrounded him, two with swords drawn, the remaining three with an arrow fitted to the string of their bows. They wore hooded cloaks, much like Alice's, that blended in with the trees. Jacob could not see their faces from the shadows cast by the hoods. They all looked exactly the same to him.

The Orn in front of Jacob put away his sword and, pulling back his hood, took a step closer. His hair was long and light, his pointed ears poked out through it, and his face was hairless and beautiful. He smiled at Jacob.

"Are you the nine-fingered boy?" he asked, smiling even bigger as he said it. It seemed to him that he was in on a joke, Jacob being the object of it.

In response, Jacob simply held up his right hand so all could see his missing finger. He felt no fear; he simply felt that he had to prove himself to them.

The smile left the Orn's face. "Are you not afraid, boy?" he asked, leaning down to Jacob's level.

Jacob shook his head.

"I am Pan, Captain of the Orn Warriors," said the Orn. The other Orns beat their chests in unison when he said it.

The Orn stood full, his eyes never leaving Jacob. "Grab him," he said and two of the Orn Warriors grabbed Jacob's arms. They led him into the Goldwood Forest.

The forest was quiet as the procession marched through the woods. Pan led the way through the forest, while the two Orns not holding Jacob flanked the group, bows and arrows at the ready.

At long last, they came to the lake. It was bigger than Jacob remembered, and he gaped at the enormous size of the lake. The trees surrounded it, but the lake itself was open to the sky, the only part of the forest the sun could penetrate.

Pan led Jacob straight toward the lake. Jacob had the sudden suspicion that they were going to toss him into the water. His heart began to race. "If they throw me in, how am I going to get back home?" Jacob wondered.

I don't know. Good luck. His brother was so helpful in times like these.

As they neared the lake, Jacob saw that a small boat rested on the shore, the waves rocking it playfully. He felt amazing relief. Whatever happened, at least he didn't have to try to swim back home.

When they reached the boat, the Orns put Jacob inside. Pan turned back to the Orn Warriors. "Return to your posts, and I will handle him on my own."

They nodded their understanding, and turned to leave. Pan grabbed one before he could get too far and spoke where Jacob could not hear. "Treefall, get to Treetop City before me and warn the Tribesmen of our arrival. I want them to be ready to deal with the boy as soon as we get there."

"Yes, Captain." Treefall said before turning away and disappearing into the depths of the forest.

Pan pushed the boat off the shore and jumped in. He grabbed an oar and began to paddle toward the other side of the lake.

"Can you tell me where you're taking me?" Jacob asked after a few moments of silence.

"No, I cannot." Pan faced the front of the boat, refusing to look at Jacob.

"But please, sir, I must know where you're taking me."

He sighed. "Boy, be still. You will know soon enough."

The two sailed on across the lake silently. Jacob's mind raced with questions, but he didn't voice any just yet. It wasn't until they reached the shore that he let a large curiosity burst.

"Can you tell me about magic?" He was thinking about what happened in the King's hall.

"There is none. Magic has gone with the colors of this land," Pan answered, his voice thick with sadness.

"But something happened earlier that can only be explained as magic."

"Boy, listen to me," Pan suddenly turned to Jacob, rage etching every line of his face, "there is no more magic. Whatever Alice told you to bring you here is foolishness. You cannot believe in magic in these lands. They're as barren as your own."

Jacob started to protest, but Pan pushed him in the back, forcing him to move along. They walked on and on, and Jacob's legs became very tired. He felt as if he hadn't rested for many days. He couldn't tell what time of day it was because the thickness of the trees blocked out all traces of the sun. And on they walked. Pan was relentless in getting them to their destination before he would let them rest.

Finally, just as Jacob felt his legs were going to quit working, Pan said, "Stop. We'll rest here for the night. Our city lies just over that hill there, but it is senseless to go that far tonight. The night securities will already be in place, so we will rest here."

Jacob lay on the cold, hard ground. He hadn't noticed how cold the air was inside the forest while he was walking all day, but now that he rested, he felt the bitter chill of the lack of sunlight under the canopy of trees. He began to shiver but sleep overtook him almost immediately.

He felt that only minutes went by when Pan was shaking him to wake him up. "Boy, it's time I take you to the Treetop City."

"So that is where you're leading me."

"Let's get moving."

He stood, and Pan led him along a well worn path through the trees. Jacob couldn't see any sign of foot prints as the Orns were soft walkers, but even his untrained eye could notice the eventual wear down of the dirt and tree roots along the way. This road had been traveled many times by many Orns.

They walked over the hill Pan mentioned the night before. As soon as Jacob cleared the ridge, he expected to see a large village splayed out before him, but instead, he saw only more trees. His heart fell when he didn't see any sign of a village for as far as his eye could see. His legs were sore and he didn't want to walk ever again.

Pan led on. They walked another mile when he stopped and looked down at Jacob. "We've arrived. We will go up to meet with the Tribesmen. I will take you personally. You will be charged with coming to our world unasked..."

"But I was asked," Jacob interrupted.

"By a child. You will probably be sent to the East. I only hope I'm not forced to take you there."

"Where is the village? I can't see anything."

"You should look up," Pan said, before walking to one of the largest trees nearby.

He looked up at the branches that were high above him. He could barely make out the bottoms of roads in the trees above. He stood with his neck craned all the way back, staring at the space above him, trying to see the village of the Orns, until Pan interrupted him. "Come on, boy. Let's move."

Jacob looked back to where Pan stood next to the giant tree trunk. The trunk itself could have easily been forty feet in diameter and probably belonged to one of the tallest trees in the forest. He was amazed to see Pan standing in the tree itself.

Jacob, too amazed to say anything, walked into the tree with Pan. The tree shut behind Jacob and sealed itself so that no one outside would be able to see the door.

"How is this happening without magic?" Jacob asked.

"It is just an old secret. Nothing more than that."

Once inside the tree, Jacob's eyes began to adjust to the lighting. Small candles lined the walls. They burned, but didn't seem to be burning, and they cast an eerie gray light around the inside of the trunk. Jacob saw that they were at the bottom of a very large stair. Winding up around the inside of the tree were hundreds of boards sticking out horizontally, making a primitive staircase. "I don't think I'll be able to make it up all those stairs," Jacob thought.

He soon realized he didn't have a choice, as Pan forced him onto the first stair. They walked up and up, higher in the tree. The burning and aching in his legs forced any other thoughts from his mind. Pan kept him marching at a brisk pace up the stairs; he didn't seem to be feeling any sort of pain from all the exercise they'd experienced the last couple of days.

When they finally reached the top, Jacob found himself standing on a platform made the same way as the stairs. Pan stepped around him and walked a few feet around the platform. He stopped and stared at the trunk. Jacob watched as he reached out with his right index finger and touched the tree. Grey sunlight began to peek through a thin line around Pan. Then a door opened.

Pan looked back at Jacob, shining brilliantly in the grey sunlight. "Are you ready, boy?" he said. Jacob simply nodded and walked out the door.

His eyes gaped as he stepped out in the noon sun. The light was grey, but the scene around him was beautiful nonetheless. He stood at the mouth of a treetop city. Great wooden roads stretched out before him. The roads made of planks were at least fifteen feet wide, and at places, narrower sidewalks broke off from the road and went straight up to porches that surrounded the trees. The trees looked misshaped as they seemed to swell into large bubbles where the porches met them. Doors and windows could be seen in the swollen trees, and Jacob realized that those were the Orns' houses. Great vines grew out of the trees and secured the roads and sidewalks in place where they weren't attached to the trees themselves.

Many Orns walked around on the roads and sidewalks, all dressed in a similar manner, much like Alice was on the day he met her, but without the color. While the sun shone down through the treetops this high up, the air was still cool, so their sleeves and cloaks made sense. Some of the Orns wore hats, some had long hair, some had short, but all were beautiful. And almost all of the Orns were women.

Pan pushed Jacob forward into the bustle of the city. "Where are all the men?" Jacob tried to ask Pan. He simply looked at Jacob and shook his head. They continued to walk.

Occasionally, an Orn-woman would greet Pan, but he just ignored them and walked on. He stared straight ahead and held onto Jacob's shoulder, as if afraid that someone would snatch him.

Jacob noticed that at different points, the sidewalks would descend down below the main road. At one point, they neared the edge of the road, and he ventured a quick peak over the edge. He was amazed to see another road stretching out under the one they were on. The city was bigger than he'd imagined.

Jacob watched one Orn-woman sitting outside of one of the trees making arrows. She had a pile of sticks that she carved into straight shafts, and fitted with sharpened rock and bone. Then he noticed that most of the trees along the road featured many more Orn-women fashioning weapons. He saw one Orn-woman making bows, and another making spears. They were preparing for war.

The road opened before Jacob and Pan, and Jacob saw the most amazing tree yet. The tree stood in the very center of the road. The tree itself was even greater than the one they'd used as stairs, wider and somewhat taller, but it ballooned out to an even greater size directly in front of where the two stood, at least three times the size of any of the houses. Stairs led up from the road up to the side of the swollen tree. Two guards stood at the bottom of the stairs.

"Are the Tribesmen waiting?" Pan asked the guards.

"Yes, sir," said the one on the right. "Treefall arrived this morning with your message." He looked down at Jacob as he finished his sentence. "So, this is the mighty hero?"

"Leave him alone, Ludlum." Pan led Jacob past the guards and up the stairs. The door opened as soon as Pan reached the top stair. He walked through the doorway, and Jacob followed.

He crossed the threshold and descended yet more stairs until he was on the floor of the swollen tree. He found himself in the scariest place he'd been in Toratoga, aside from the King's presence. In the very center of the room was a fire pit, burning a small grey fire. On the opposite side of the fire were nine people sitting at a curved table that seemed to grow right out of the tree itself. Strange smoke filled the room and fogged Jacob's vision. The door closed and sealed behind him, so that the only light in the room was from the fire.

Shadows danced across the Tribesmen and around the room. Jacob could just make out the silhouettes of guards along the wall. Pan grabbed his shoulder and pulled him up to the fire pit.

"I, Pan of Goldwood, have brought the Tribesmen the nine-fingered boy. We found him yesterday strolling into the forest with a Grebble..."

"I was not with a Grebble," Jacob interrupted. Pan nodded at a guard to his right. The guard stepped up to Jacob and tied a gag around his mouth. He said no more while Pan spoke.

"As I was saying," continued Pan, "we found him with a Grebble. The boy told the Grebble to go elsewhere while he entered the forest. He appeared to show no fear as he prepared to march into the wood. We killed the Grebble, and the boy was surrounded. I have personally brought him here, as was your request."

Jacob couldn't believe what he was hearing. He would have raised his outrage if not for the gag around his mouth. His rage conquered his fear.

"Pan, tell me," said the center Tribesman. In the dim light, Jacob could just see a few of the features of a very old Orn sitting behind the table, in the center. He had long hair and a smooth beard with two streaks running down it like very long fangs. He had his hood pulled around his head, so these were the only features Jacob could see. "How was it that this boy was coming into the forest? We know that Alice informed him on how to get into our world, so he had to come in through Kelpie Lake. How did he escape detection?"

"Sir, our defenses were interrupted by the return of Alice into our world. As you know, Alice caused us some problems before we brought her to you. The boy must have slipped into our world while we were dealing with her. We did not know when he would arrive."

Jacob gave a silent cheer to Alice for putting up a fight.

"But where did he go, Pan?" the Orn asked again. He was clearly the leader of the Tribesmen.

"I do not know, sir," Pan said.

"You did not think to ask him?"

"No, sir, I thought I would leave that up to you."

Jacob reached behind his head and began to work the knot of the gag that was tied around his head. He'd not been good with knots since the loss of his finger, but he worked it out easily enough. As soon as the gag was removed, he said, "If you want to know where I went, I will tell you."

The Tribesmen grew very quiet, and Pan looked down at the boy, shocked that he'd made a noise. "You should wait to speak until you are asked to speak," the Tribesman said.

"I don't know why I should treat you with respect when you've done little to treat me well. I simply came into this world to try to help save it, and I have had nothing but trouble ever since I first arrived. I would return home, but I do not know the way."

The mood in the room seemed to change after Jacob's speech. Everything went quiet and Jacob, too, was impressed with what he'd said. The Tribesmen, save the middle one, looked around uncomfortably. Jacob realized that no one had talked so outwardly toward the Tribesmen before him. He wondered what fate would befall him now.

The elderly Orn stood and pressed his hands into the table. His face remained in shadow. "Welcome to the council of the Tribesmen, Jacob Nine-fingers. I am Galadawn, director of the Tribesmen and leader of the free Orns of the Goldwood Forest. As you can see, there are nine of us Tribesmen. The four to my right are Nora, Seraglio, Donner, and Flora. To my left are Sasol, Namely, Ezra, and of course, Elda."

Each Orn nodded in Jacob's direction at the mention of their names. Elda pulled her own hood back so Jacob could see her face. She was older, perhaps older than anyone he'd ever known. Lines decorated every inch of her face, and all of her hair was gone. Her eyes were entirely white, and Jacob realized that she must be blind.

"You have no doubt been summoned here by Alice," Galadawn continued. "She is a most peculiar Orn-child and acts greatly on instinct. I think Elda knew that and used it to her advantage when she told the child of the prophecy. We have dealt with Alice properly, according to our laws. Do not worry, child, you will see her shortly.

"Now tell us, Jacob Nine-fingers, where did you go after you left the lake?"

Jacob didn't hesitate, he stood there proudly among those who would doubt him, and he told his tale. He told the Orn Tribesmen all about meeting William, about his ride to the black castle, and about his encounter with King Ro, giving only enough detail for them to know that Aural was there. When he at last told of the death of Aural, the room fell silent, and Jacob waited for what would come next.

"So, Aural is fallen then?" Galadawn asked.

"Yes," Jacob said. Tears stung the corners of his eyes at the memory of the Orn. He enjoyed her company, though he knew her only a short while. "The king killed her on the field. There was nothing I could do against his soldiers and Grebbles."

Each Orn took a moment to mourn the loss of Aural. Finally, Galadawn broke the silence again. "Aural was one of our greatest spies. She gave us many details about the enemy," he said. "And she was a firm believer in the prophecy."

Jacob stared through the flames at the small Orn who was still standing behind the table. "Do you mean," he began, "that there are some who don't believe in the prophecy?"

Galadawn sighed. "I am afraid there is only one in this room, aside from yourself, who believes the prophecy. And that, of course, is the woman who made the prophecy in the first place."

Jacob stared at the Orn. "You don't believe?" he said. The horror of it all began to fall heavily onto his shoulders.

If they don't believe then what will happen to us?

As if reading his thought, Galadawn said, "We will vote on what will happen to you. Your tale of what you have done so far while in Toratoga is astounding. I personally don't believe half of it. No child could face King Ro, the most evil ruler of our time, and live to tell about it.

"Tribesmen," he said, looking to either side of him. "We have a decision to make. Who wants to send him across the sea?"

But before any could raise a hand to vote, Elda stood. "Wait one moment, Galadawn," she said. Her voice was small but very commanding. Everyone in the room looked to her. Jacob's heart leapt, knowing that she would save him from this mess. "What if the boy can perform magic?"

"Magic?" Galadawn scoffed. "None can perform magic in this land anymore, you know that."

"But what if *he* can?"

"I don't know. I guess that would prove your prophecy, would it not?"

Elda turned from him and faced Jacob's direction. "Jacob," she said, "when you were in the king's chamber, how did you manage to free Aural without the king noticing?"

"Elda, this is ridiculous, we have no proof that he even went to the black castle," Galadawn interrupted. "For all we know, Aural is still at her post, spying."

"But I did," Jacob said. "If I didn't meet Aural then how would I know her name?"

Galadawn began to respond, but wasn't able to think of anything to say. He sat down and let Elda have control of the floor.

Jacob continued, "I was just concentrating on the knife the king handed me. It began to burn in my hand, and then everything stopped moving, like time was standing still. I cut the ropes from Aural, and everything returned to normal."

Elda smiled. "I thought something like that may have happened. Jacob, that was magic. Or at least a very advanced form of it. For some of the more powerful magic wielders, it was possible to freeze time to see the true essence of everything around them. I cannot be sure of how it happened, maybe you brought some magic back from your own land, but it did happen."

"That was magic?" Jacob asked, looking down at his hands in amazement.

"Well, yes," said Elda.

"This still does not prove anything," Galadawn said, once more standing behind the table. He reached into his pocket and pulled a small purple feather from it. The color caught the attention of everyone in the room. "If you've done it once, you can do it again. Freeze time and take this feather from my hand."

"I don't even know how I did it," Jacob said and when he saw Galadawn move to replace the feather, he added, "But I will try."

Jacob closed his eyes and concentrated hard. He tried to imagine himself back at the castle, standing before the king, but nothing happened. He tried harder, but he could not get time to stop; he could not freeze the moment. At long last he opened his eyes.

"Ah, you see, fellow Tribesmen, he has no power," Galadawn said, putting the feather back into his pocket. "If he was able to perform some slight bit of magic it was all he brought with him into our world. He has no powers now. There is no magic in this land."

Jacob looked pleadingly to Elda, but she returned to her seat, shaking her head. He looked up to Pan and was not surprised to see him smiling.

They hate you. You have to get out of there, Taylor said.

"We will now vote on whether or not we should send you away," Galadawn said.

"Please," Jacob pleaded, feeling the tears well up in his eyes. "Can't I just go home?"

"No, child, I am sorry, but our laws prohibit that. You came here, and you will die here. Now, vote. Who wants to send him across the sea?"

Jacob's heart plummeted as eight hands went into the air. All of them except Elda's.

"The Tribesmen have decided," Galadawn concluded. "You, child, will be taken to the beach with the other prisoners and wait for the boat to take you across the sea. I had a feeling you would see Alice again.

"Council dismissed."

At that, everyone stood from their seats and exited through a door behind their table. As the moisture pooled in his eyes, Jacob felt the sting of rejection and the sorrow that came with it.

"Come on, boy, I guess I will take you," Pan said beside him. And without looking up, Jacob turned to follow him out into the afternoon sunlight and toward his doom.

Chapter 8

A Small Hope

Jacob's heart broke.

He'd gone through so much already just to save this world and now he was being thrown away like some old, dirty rag. His eyes were wet with tears as Pan led him back through the city toward the stairs. His heart was burdened with the sadness that he would never see his mother again, never see home again, and anger wrenched at his insides just thinking about the Tribesmen.

Where was the magic? Even the voice of his brother had no affect on his sadness.

Before Jacob noticed, they had descended the last stair and were exiting the tree. They headed immediately to the east, Jacob keeping his head down, watching his feet walk over the grey earth. Pan walked slowly next to him, giving him the time to overcome his grief and anger. He'd escorted many prisoners to the beach before this, and most of them had the same reactions of sadness and anger.

The sun fell below the horizon and made the already dark forest even darker. Jacob was having a tough time seeing Pan in front of him. The trees were so much thicker here than everywhere else he'd walked.

"Jacob, let's stop and rest for the night," Pan finally said, after Jacob nearly fell over a huge tree root. The fact that Pan used his name for the first time was not lost on Jacob, but he was still too depressed to comment on it. He'd been so sure that when it came down to it, he would be accepted into the Orn community, and he would save their world.

"Okay," Jacob replied.

Pan gathered some wood and made a fire. He hunted a plump rabbit, cleaned it, and began cooking it. Jacob sat close to the fire, letting the flames warm his cold body. When the sun went down, the temperature in the forest dropped with it.

"Did you really face the king?" Pan asked after they'd sat, quietly eating for a few moments.

Without looking up from his food, he replied, "Yes. Why would I lie about that? What did I gain from it?"

Pan, thinking the same thing, responded, "Nothing, nothing at all. That's why I thought you might have been telling the truth."

Jacob looked up, surprised. "You...you believe me?"

"Uh...I think maybe I do."

"Then we have to go back, you have to tell Galadawn." Jacob jumped to his feet to stress the importance of this revelation. His food lay at his feet, forgotten for the moment.

"Whoa, Jacob, settle down. If I did that, I could lose my rank, and I might even end up crossing the sea with you. That would do neither of us any good."

His hope faded. "Yeah, I guess I see your point."

"I'll tell you a secret. Before the fall of the king and imminent destruction of Toratoga, I could wield magic. None know of my ability because magic became such a fear to the king that it was outlawed. I dared not expose myself to anyone, not even my kinsmen.

"The days following King Ro's fall were dark. None suspected that evil had arisen in him. It had been so long since the last fallen king. And not many spend time reading the histories these days or maybe we would have seen the signs.

"Magic wielders were killed off, and I became afraid for my own life. I kept my secret hidden, and as the land began to destroy itself, my power began to fade.

"But I still know the secrets to magic wielding.

"No one else in the Tribesmen Council knows about the secrets of magic. Because I do, I knew that you were telling the truth when you told of your experience in the King's chamber. They have heard stories, which is why they thought they could test you.

"I don't know how you did it, but I think Galadawn was wrong when he said that you used the magic you brought here with you. I think the magic came from the knife. I don't know why, but you said the knife became hot in your hand. That must have been the magic transferring to you."

Jacob couldn't believe what he was hearing. A thousand questions tumbled through his head all at once. He asked the most important one. "Why couldn't I do any magic in front of the Tribesmen?"

"For one thing, you used up the magic from the knife and did not know how to get anymore. You would be able to if you worked at it hard enough or if someone trained you."

"So you mean if I am trained, I will be able to perform that trick again?"

"That trick and many, many more, much more amazing than that."

"Will you teach me?"

The question caught Pan off guard. "What? I can't. You are a prisoner and I am your guard. I can't just teach you magic. You'd be able to escape from the beach and cause all kinds of problems for us."

His excitement building, Jacob once more stood. "Pan, you must. You believe my story, you believe I can do magic. But I can't do any without your help."

"Jacob, I cannot do this," Pan shouted, also jumping to his feet. "It would undermine the authority of the Tribesmen."

"Please, Pan, this is my only hope."

Pan stared at the boy, fighting his urge to help him. He was the Captain of the Orn Warriors for a reason and this boy would not spoil that. "You cannot ask this of me, Jacob."

"But...what if I am the only hope of the Goldwood Forest? Your home?"

Jacob asked the right question. Pan decided that he must help Jacob because of the prophecy; he knew that Jacob was telling the truth and that he must be the last hope for the forest and all of Toratoga. Plus, he was a rule breaker himself when he learned magic. "All right," he said. "I will show you what I can tonight, but I must take you on to the beach tomorrow and leave you there. If you are able to escape, you can find your way back to the Treetop City."

"What do I do?"

"My magical abilities are very limited. What you described in the king's castle is advanced magic. I think that may be why most of the Tribesmen didn't believe you. Not many people can freeze time. From what I've read on the subject, your description was perfect. Even though I can't do it, I did read how to do it.

"When you seize the moment, you will see the way everything really looks. Nothing can conceal itself from you while you are in that state. You will find that fire is no longer hot, and that the forest is no longer cold. Everything goes to neutral when you enter that state.

"You must seize this moment in your mind. Close your eyes and concentrate on plucking this moment, like you would a feather from a chicken. You will be able to hold it for a few minutes, but with your limited strength, it will soon end. Give it a try."

Jacob closed his eyes and tried to visualize taking the moment. He bent his entire will towards seizing time where it stood. Nothing seemed to be happening. At last, he opened his eyes, giving in to defeat and was shocked to see the world of color like he saw in King Ro's castle.

The fire sat, not moving on the charred logs. Jacob gasped as he saw that the trees around him were now a deep gold with silver leaves clinging to each branch. Pan looked at him with a small smile on his face. His bright green eyes, illuminated by the fire but oddly still, looked right at Jacob. Jacob stood and walked right up to Pan when he lost the moment.

His vision began to shake and the color slipped from all his surroundings. Pan jumped back in surprised when he saw how close Jacob stood to him. To Jacob, the moment had stretched on allowing him to walk the few paces to Pan, but to Pan, it had only been a moment, as fast as the blink of an eye. One second Jacob was sitting across the fire from him, the next he was standing right in front of his face.

Pan laughed, "You did it."

"Yeah, but not for very long," Jacob said. He wasn't surprised at all that he'd accomplished the feat again, but he was disappointed that it hadn't lasted long.

"Just the fact that you can do it is incredible. Have patience: the stronger you get the longer you will be able to hold it. It takes practice and patience."

"Okay, but how do I get more magic?"

"Everything in nature has magic contained inside of it. Some more than others. You just have to touch the object and enter it with your mind. If you earn the trust of the object, you will gain its magic. You show the land and its inhabitants that you mean no harm, and they will gladly lend you their powers."

"Now you can absorb magic from anything that has it. I will tell you that the trees of the Goldwood Forest are some of the most magical things you will find in this world. Simply put your hand on it. To use it, focus all your energy into what you want the magic to do. Whatever you want to happen will happen."

"I should try to do something then," Jacob said.

"Not tonight, I'm afraid. You've had a tasking day already, and further attempting magic could kill you. You don't want to do more than your strength allows. You will know your own limits eventually. Now off to bed."

And all at once Jacob did feel very tired. Lying back on the ground, he fell instantly asleep. It seemed only minutes before Pan woke him up. He couldn't believe it was time to get up, but a little sunlight trickled down through the trees to light the forest.

"Get up," Pan said. "We must get to the beach. The ship to take you to Eastern shore should arrive today."

Jacob got to his feet and felt the tightness in his heart. He didn't know if he'd be able to escape the beach or if he would at least be able to help Alice escape. His heart hammered harder in his chest when he thought of Alice. Her eyes haunted him constantly, somewhere between every thought. His nerves scrambled as he thought of seeing her again.

Pan led Jacob through the forest. An occasional whistle let Pan know that the forest guard were near by and watching out for him. He wouldn't respond; he just continued to walk toward the east.

By midday, they arrived at the break in the trees. Jacob, having seen the ocean hundreds of times in South Carolina, recognized the scent of the water and heard the crashing as the waves hit the shore. The trees parted and revealed a miserable grey sea stretching out to the horizon. He couldn't believe how sad the water looked without its color. The air coming off the water pierced the skin with its cold arrows.

Two human soldiers walked up to Pan when he stepped onto the beach. They still wore their uniforms from King Ro's army.

"You have a new prisoner," Pan said when they reached him. "He is to go to the East with the others. Watch him."

The soldiers grabbed Jacob and pulled him out onto the beach. Pan stood watching but showed no emotion. He was sure he would see the boy again. He watched until the soldiers threw Jacob in the huddle with the other prisoners and turned back to the forest.

As soon as Jacob reached the group of people surrounding a small fire, Alice jumped up and wrapped her arms around his neck.

"You came," she said, breathless and a huge smile on her face. Jacob was surprised to see the changes in her features from the lack of color.

"Of course, I did," he responded.

"Are you here to rescue me?"

He simply shook his head and told her how the Tribesmen sent him here to go off to the East with her. Her smile faltered and sadness built up through her features.

"But how could they possibly send you here?" she asked at the end of his tale.

"I was wondering why they would send *you* here."

"Well, I didn't really have permission to travel into another world. They knew why I went, you see, and so I was deemed a danger to the Goldwood Forest. I never worried, though, because I had your promise that you would come to save us."

"I would like to, honestly, but with the way I've been treated since I came here, I don't know that I want to."

Alice let out a gasp and stared at him, dumbstruck.

"I mean I want to help *you*," Jacob continued. "Of course I do, but I guess I just miss home."

"Don't you see, Jacob, that I miss my home, too? This world is nothing like the world I used to live in. The evil has destroyed everything good about it. I want to see the trees with their golden hue and silver leaves, and I want to see that vast expanse of desert to be trees again. I want the evil to be gone, and you are my only hope for that." Tears began to run down Alice's cheeks, and Jacob felt her pain as he watched the tears roll down her cheeks.

He made the decision that he would rescue her from the beach and they would travel back to the Treetop City together. And in that moment, something inside Jacob, perhaps just seeing the tears of the beautiful Alice, turned him from the little boy of Abbey, Oklahoma, to a man, the man who would save Toratoga from its own destruction. Alice saw the change come over his face and at once dried her tears.

"Alice, do you know how to get back to the city?" he asked her.

"It's straight west from here. But, Jacob we can't fight these soldiers."

"We won't have to. Not if I can do a little magic."

Alice eyes grew enormous. "Can you really?"

He ran to a nearby tree and placed his hand on the bark. He closed his eyes and could feel the pulse of tree inside his head, could hear its voice deep within. He made a silent promise to the tree to do no harm, only good with the power it gave him. He felt a rush of green light run through his fingertips, his arm, and through his whole body. He took his hand away from the tree, feeling that new power course through his body like blood, and went back to Alice.

"Take my hand," he said, holding out his hand to her. She grabbed it, and Jacob felt her smooth skin in his own. He completely forgot about the cold.

He closed his eyes and concentrated on the moment. With everything in him, he seized it. When he opened his eyes, everything was once again frozen, everything but

Alice. She looked about at the change in Toratoga and gasped.

"Jacob, what is this?"

"We don't have time for explanations right now. I can only hold it for a little while."

And they ran. The frozen soldiers never saw them leave. Only later when the ship arrived to take the prisoners to the East did they notice that the small boy Pan had brought that day was gone. In their panic, they chose not to report the missing child.

But once back in the forest, Jacob had to worry about the forest guard keeping watch in the trees. He pulled Alice down low to the ground with him when he lost the moment and time resumed. He felt a shudder go through Alice as the trees changed back.

He scanned the trees, hoping for a glimpse of one of the Orn Warriors, but there was nothing.

"Jacob, what happened?" Alice asked. "Why isn't anyone chasing us? And how did the colors come back?"

"Hasn't anyone ever told you about magic?" Jacob asked.

"No. They're forbidden to give out its secrets by the Tribesmen."

"I could have guessed as much, but right now, we need to worry about the Warriors. They are probably up in the trees and we need to get back to the Treetop City without their help."

"The guard usually doesn't come out this far. At least, I can't remember them ever coming out here."

"They were above us when Pan was bringing me to the beach. I heard their whistles."

"They follow Pan, of course, he's their leader. They were probably just watching to make sure he was safe."

"Then why would they whistle and give away that they were there. And why would they follow him when I'm just some lousy kid?"

"There are other dangers in these woods other than you, Jacob. When Pan is sent some place, scouts go out ahead of him to make sure the danger is minimal. A whistle means everything ahead is clear. A blast from the horn is danger."

"How do you know all of this?" Jacob asked, his eyebrows arching and his eyes investigating her features.

"My sister Aural is a spy for the guard. She was a part of the Warriors before they sent her to spy on the king."

Jacob felt his heart fall down to rest behind his belly button. He didn't want to have to be the one to tell Alice that her sister died. "Aural?" he asked. "She was your sister?"

She tilted her head toward him. "Yes, she is my sister. Why? Did you meet her?"

He couldn't run away from it; he had to tell Alice about her sister. "Yes, Alice, I met her. Now I understand why she was so determined to believe that Jacob Nine-fingers would save her. You both have such faith in me."

A smile bent up the corners of Alice's mouth. "Where did you meet her? Is she back home, then?"

Jacob sighed deeply and told her about his adventure to the black castle and the fall of Aural. The evidence of Alice's heartbreaking showed up on her face as it crumpled with Jacob's story and fell into a huge sobbing mess. Tears streamed down her face and Jacob was eerily reminded of the blood running down Aural's face, like the last tear of a good hard cry.

Awkwardly, he put his arms around her and held her to him while she cried. He could do no more than rock her gently, stroke her hair, and whisper sweet phrases in her ear. Eventually, she calmed, the sobs coming slower and slower, until they stopped altogether. She lifted her head and looked into his eyes, and for an instant, he thought that they'd regained their color. But after he blinked, he saw that he'd been mistaken. They were still colorless, although, no longer dull.

"And the Odds came down to get her?" Alice asked, her voice barely more than a whisper.

"What are the Odds?" Jacob asked.

"Oh I forget that you know nothing of this world. They are blue women, a combination of spirit and light. They dwell in In-Between; they come to take those who die in Toratoga to In-Between where the bodies rest before their spirit continues on to Elsewhere."

Jacob had a vivid recollection of the lights that took the form of women when they landed and carried Aural's body away. "Yes, that must have been them," he told her.

"I guess she's all right then."

"She did what she could to save me. Come on, Alice, we need to hurry."

The sun began to fall farther in the distant horizon, and the darkness swept through the forest once again, faster than a mouse escaping its predator. Alice and Jacob ran through the forest, bounding between the trees, dodging low hanging branches and nearly stumbling over the massive roots of the trees. They ran on well after the sun went down, determined to see the Treetop City before the sun made its ascent back into the sky.

92

Jacob felt his head pounding, his lungs working overtime to get the air his body demanded. His legs struggled to keep up with the stronger Orn running in front of him, leading the way to her home. Just as the sun began to whisper the dawn's name on the horizon, Alice stopped running. She'd spotted the torches of Treetop City high up in the trees.

Jacob bent over and panted for air; he felt relief swarm over him after running so far. They'd made it, and not one soldier had given chase to the two fugitives. They neared the stairs that he and Pan had taken to City, and just as they reached the base of the great tree, a voice spoke out.

"Jacob," it said.

Jacob felt his heart break; they'd been caught after coming this far. Someone was watching for them, and now they were trapped.

Chapter 9

A Second Council

Jacob turned back and saw Pan come out from the shadows. Alice jumped beside Jacob and prepared for an attack. She'd had enough experience with Pan so far to know what he would do now that he'd caught them. Jacob hadn't told her about Pan believing the Prophecy.

"It's all right, Alice," Jacob said, holding out his hand to her. "He's okay."

Alice stopped her advance on Pan and stared at Jacob. "How can you say that?" she asked. "He's the one who captured me."

"Yes, I know. He captured me, too," Jacob responded. "But he also taught me the basics of magic before releasing me to the guards of the beach."

Pan stood silent listening to this, but finally he spoke. "Jacob, we must hurry. The guard will not attack you while I am with you, unless given a specific order by the Tribesmen. I can get you out of the forest."

Jacob turned his gaze from Alice to Pan, suddenly feeling the weight of his words before he spoke them. "Pan, I must return the Treetop City."

"No, you fool!" Pan exclaimed, raising his voice slightly. "To reenter the city is death. If you can save us, that isn't the way."

"If I don't return to the city, to the Tribesmen, how can they even trust me? And how can I save them if they don't trust me? This is a war, Pan, we must fight together or there is no hope."

Pan looked at the boy, mesmerized by his words. The eagerness he'd seen in the boy by the fire while discussing magic had been replaced by the boldness of a warrior who faced certain death. He looked at him and knew in his heart that he would follow this boy anywhere, to the very frontlines of battle.

Pan nodded his consent, and Jacob turned to Alice, "Are you with us?" he asked her.

Her smile lit the gloom in the shade of the trees. "I risked death just to find you," she said. "This is nothing."

And so, the three of them climbed the stairs up to the Treetop City. The morning sun began to cast its light through the trees and onto the roads where Jacob, Alice and Pan walked, making their way toward the center of the city, in hopes of finding council.

No citizens walked the streets of the city in the early light of the morning, save for a few soldiers who looked surprised to see Pan walking with these two known criminals. Some made advancements toward Pan, but he held his palm up to them, stopping them in their tracks. At last they reached the hall of the Tribesmen.

"Ludlum, are the Tribesmen here?" Pan asked the guard on the left.

"No, sir, today is the ceremony, and they are preparing for it," the guard answered him.

"Will you send someone to meet us in the hall?"

"Sir?"

"We seek council with the Tribesmen, Ludlum. Will you send someone to retrieve them for us?"

"Sir, I will go myself if you will permit it."

"Yes, go then, but make it quick."

"And what should I tell them this concerns?"

"Ludlum, open your eyes! You see who I have standing here with me. Now go!"

Ludlum did not wait any longer, but ran off around the hall in search of the Tribesmen. The other guard at the door remained silent as Pan led Alice and Jacob into the hall. The small fire in the center continued to burn and gave the hall some grey light.

"This is madness, Jacob," Pan said, once they were inside the hall. "We can still make a run for it."

"You know it's too late for that, Pan," Jacob replied. He felt nervousness well up inside of him. He had a strange confidence that the Tribesmen would believe him and he would be able to remain among them to prepare for the battle.

Thoughts of battle made his nerves creep even more. No matter what sort of confidence he displayed on the outside, on the inside he felt he'd never be able to achieve the greatness Alice and Pan thought him capable of. He was still just a little boy and nothing more than that, most of the time.

At long last the back door to the hall opened, and nine Orns, silhouetted by the sun, entered the room; the last of these was Galadawn, bent with age, hobbling to his chair. The door closed behind them, and each took their seat behind the table.

"What is this about?" Galadawn asked.

"Sir," Pan began, "I just wanted to bring these two here today—"

"What do you mean by bringing two convicted criminals into our hall?" Galadawn interrupted him.

"Sir, I only wanted to give them one more chance to plead their case," Pan said.

But before any of the Tribesmen could respond, everything froze. Jacob opened his eyes and saw why the Tribesmen chose to meet in this hall. It was full of color and easily the most luxurious building he'd yet seen in Toratoga, but he had no time to stare about. He bent quickly and placed his palms on the floor. His mind went into the tree. He felt every leaf moving in the wind. He felt water being pulled up through the roots to spread throughout the limbs. And he felt the magic.

The tree acknowledged his presence. "Who are you, boy?" A deep voice echoed through his head.

"I am Jacob, and I am trying to save this world. But I need your help."

"You are human. Yet you feel stranger than most. Should I trust you with my magic?"

"I will not harm you or any Orn. I just want to save you."

"Yes, I see the truth in what you say. Your mind is open to me. Your courage is compelling. Take what you can."

A green light filled his vision and a tingling sensation began in his fingertips and ran up through his body. His palms began to burn, and he released them. He stood up in the same spot he'd been in, so that none would notice, and he released the moment.

"Pan, you are treading on grounds for dismissal. You have worked hard your whole life to obtain the position you are in, and yet you throw it away for some human boy and a foolish girl," Galadawn continued on as if nothing had happened, just as Jacob hoped.

"There is too much left undone by simply sending them away for such foolishness," Pan said, his voice building, and his cheeks flushing. "How can you explain away the fact that Jacob knew—"

"We will not be spoken to like that," interrupted a pretty blond Orn on Galadawn's right named Flora.

Pan quieted but gave a heavy sigh.

"You have brought us here on the day of ceremony," Flora continued. "And now we must pass a judgment on *you*."

"On me?" Pan asked, a small plea in his voice. "But I've done nothing."

"Correction," Galadawn began, standing up from his chair, "You know the importance of this day, and you know punishment for helping known criminals escape their prison." He leaned onto the table, supporting his weight on his long, boney fingers.

Seraglio, a large rough looking Orn, stood up on Galadawn's right. "Ludlum," he shouted, "bring your guards and take these three away."

The door behind Jacob, Alice, and Pan opened at once, and six guards rushed into the hall. Jacob, knowing that things were getting bad, reserved his strength for just this moment.

When the six guards neared them, he thrust his hands out to either side of his body and concentrated hard on throwing the magic he'd absorbed from the tree out of his body and into the oncoming guards. He didn't know what would happen, but he felt this was the way to go about it. A great green mist rushed through every part of his body and almost caused him to lose his balance. It launched out of him in the exact form of his body and hit the oncoming guards.

The effect was just what Jacob wanted. All of the guards were thrown back into the wall of the hall and knocked unconscious.

After the magic exited his body, Jacob bent forward, panting. He felt suddenly very weak, and his legs gave out so that he went down to his knees. The Tribesmen were all standing now, all shouting at different levels about what they'd just seen. Alice fell to Jacob's side to give him comfort, while Pan took the time to find his voice.

"Tribesmen, you can now see how wrong you were," he said to the nine Orns standing in front of him. They quieted, listening to what the captain had to say. "Jacob just performed magic for your proof, and the effort has nearly killed him. Allow me to train this boy, the way Orn Warriors are trained and he will lead us to victory in the fight against King Ro."

Galadawn, appearing to have become too weak to stand, sat back in his chair. He studied the boy with hard eyes. He was overcome with what he'd just seen, and Pan waited for the leader's response.

"I refuse to believe that this is any kind of proof that this boy should not be sent away," Galadawn finally said. An audible gasp filled the room at his words, and all heads turned to look at him, all except for Jacob who continued lying on the floor, working to regain his breath.

"You cannot be serious," Pan shouted.

Alice stood, saying, "How can you still not believe?"

"I am afraid that, as impressive as that trick was, our law is very strict concerning people from other worlds coming here," Galadawn said. "We must do what we Orns have promised to do."

"As my eyes have failed me, I did not quite see what happened," the tired voice of Elda came from the far end of the table. "But I felt it, Jacob, and no longer should there be any doubt that you are the One to save us." She smiled in his direction, and Jacob looked up at her.

With help from Pan and Alice, Jacob stood up on his unsteady legs. He looked at each of the Tribesmen in turn, noticing the rings on their right index fingers for the first time. They were identical to the one Alice wore and the mangled one he kept in his pocket.

Finally he spoke, "I only came here to help. Permit me to at least try; no harm will come to you for that. Or if that is too much to ask, permit me to return home, where I can live a normal life and forget all about Toratoga."

"If you go home, you will want to return," said Ezra, a small female Orn sitting next to Elda.

"Yes, we have seen it before," spoke the Orn woman sitting next to Galadawn named Nora. "Many will come to our world, only to find that its memory haunts them once they return to their own."

"If many have come here and been allowed to leave, why am I treated like your greatest enemy?" Jacob asked. He could feel his strength building.

"Ah, well, these are dangerous times," Galadawn said. "We had to make a choice to limit the dangers in Toratoga, and we felt that allowing anyone to freely roam in and out of our world was one of the most dangerous things we've done."

"But surely you see, Galadawn, that this child has brought no danger to us," Seraglio said, looking down the table to Galadawn. "If anything we should reward him for escaping the beach without anyone being alerted to his departure."

Jacob felt warmth well up inside of him. Already he'd caused some in the room to change their beliefs about him. He waited to hear what the Tribesmen would decide to do with him.

"Come now, we must decide what to do about these three," Namely said, "The ceremony will begin soon."

"You are right," Galadawn said. "We must vote on their imprisonment."

Jacob, determined to be strong, locked eyes with Galadawn. The voting commenced, and once again, they voted eight to one. Only this time, all the Tribesmen voted against Galadawn. Jacob, Alice, and Pan were all free.

"Fine," Galadawn said, slamming his palm down on the table in front of him, showing surprising strength, "Let them go, but the fall of the Goldwood Forest will be on your hands."

"Galadawn," Elda said, "The Goldwood Forest will fall anyway."

With that, the council was adjourned when Galadawn stood from his seat and walked out the back door as fast as his old body would allow him.

"Am I allowed to give Jacob proper training, then?" Pan asked before the Tribesmen walked out the door.

"Of course," Elda said. "The prophecy can't fulfill itself. Get him a sword and clothes fit for an Orn, but make sure he comes to the ceremony."

The happiness burned in Jacob hotter than a thousand suns. He beamed at Pan and Alice. Alice pulled him into a tight hug and Pan laughed at the look on Jacob's face.

"Thank you," Jacob said when the embrace ended. "You two really stood up for me. I couldn't have done it without you."

"We have a lot of work to do, Jacob, so don't go thinking the war is over yet," Pan said. "This was just the smallest of battles."

Jacob walked out of the hall with Pan and Alice, passing the unconscious bodies of the Warriors. Once outside, he saw the Treetop City with a new eye. Everything seemed to glow in front of him. He knew in his heart that he would do all he could to save this world.

Chapter 10

The Ceremony

In high spirits, Pan took Jacob down to the second level of the city to the armory located in the tree just below the council hall. Alice went off to find her parents to let them know she was fine, but she promised that she would find them for the ceremony.

Jacob, who realized there wasn't much in the world of Toratoga that he understood, became more and more curious about the ceremony every time it was mentioned. As he walked to the armory with Pan, he ventured to ask, to which Pan responded, "You will find out soon enough. Let's worry about getting your sword first and then I can fill you in."

One of the king's guard stood watch outside the armory. Jacob stared at the man standing by the tree as if he hadn't seen another human in years. Without the stress of being taken as a prisoner, he focused on the fact that soldiers also guarded the beach. The fact that there were humans living among the Orns surprised Jacob.

"Captain," the man said to Pan as they neared.

"Arthur, this is Jacob," Pan said to the soldier named Arthur.

Arthur looked at Jacob with wide eyes, as if he needed to take in every detail of the boy and his eyes were just not large enough. "It is an honor," he said before falling to his knees in front of Jacob. Jacob looked awkwardly from Arthur to Pan.

"Stand up, Arthur," Pan said, "you're embarrassing the boy."

Finally, Arthur stood. "What can I do for you, Captain?" he asked, his eyes continuing to wander to Jacob.

"Jacob needs a sword and Orn clothes," Pan said. Arthur looked at him curiously. "I will train him as a Warrior, so he must look like one of us."

Arthur bowed to show he understood before disappearing through a door behind him. When he emerged, he held in his arms a bundle of clothes and a short sword with a belt and sheath. Jacob removed the clothes William had given him and put on his new Orn clothes. They were much like Pan's with less decoration that obviously denoted his rank.

The sleeves of the tunic fell to the middle of his forearm and the tunic fell to the middle of his thigh. His pants were tights to ensure maximum mobility. He felt warmer in these clothes that were designed for the frigid temperatures of the forest. He placed the belt around his waist, and Arthur gave him a long cloak that he clasped around his neck.

"Thank you, Arthur," Jacob said after he finished dressing.

104

Arthur again bowed low to him. He and Pan turned back to the upper level of the city. Jacob felt right at home in his new clothes, walking among the Orns dressed in the same fashion. His fingers itched to try out the sword. He and Taylor often had "sword" fights with sticks they'd find around their yard back in South Carolina.

Thinking of those happier times, he considered the reason he'd left his own world. Everything came down to a prophecy an old Orn made at some point long ago. His life was normal up until Alice broke in with life-changing news a little over a week ago.

While thinking of the prophecy, a very troubling thought occurred to him.

"Pan," he said, coming to a halt in the middle of the road. Pan stopped abruptly at the tone in Jacob's voice.

"What is it, Jacob?" Pan asked.

"It's just something Aural said after we escaped the castle," Jacob said. "She told me that only the Orns know about the prophecy. So how could King Ro know about it also?"

Jacob looked up at Pan in hopes of some comfort on this subject, but Pan simply shook his head.

"We have suspected for some time that there may be a traitor in our midst."

"You mean that an Orn has betrayed his own kind?"

Pan nodded.

"But why?"

"I don't know what gain an Orn may achieve by consorting with King Ro. I believe that, whoever it is has grown tired of the constant battles we face, and in hopes of ending this war, gave valuable information to the king."

"So you don't know who it is?"

"No, I'm afraid we don't. Your story confirmed our fear that a traitor lives among us, but we are still no closer to finding out who it is."

Jacob began walking once more, troubled with the thought of a traitor. He didn't know any of the Orns enough to be able to call one a traitor. He immediately thought of Galadawn as the traitor. Galadawn had refused to believe Jacob despite the amount of evidence he'd presented. The more Jacob thought about it, the more he became convinced that it was Galadawn.

"Do you think," Jacob began, "that the traitor could possibly be Galadawn?"

Pan's mouth fell slightly as he looked down at Jacob. "I don't think that's possible, Jacob," he said. "Why would you ask that?"

Jacob shrugged, "Just the way he's been treating me and everyone else who shows me any sort of support."

"He's just a stubborn old man, just let it go." Pan continued walking, not allowing Jacob to further question him.

Jacob, however, could not turn away from it that easily. Of course, he hadn't really met Galadawn one on one, but he still felt positive about it. *He must have thought that if King Ro couldn't get rid of us, he could simply ship us away,* Make-Believe-Taylor chimed in helpfully.

"You've been quiet lately," Jacob responded.

"What?" Pan asked as he turned back to see why Jacob spoke.

"Uh, nothing," he responded. Pan gave him a hard stare for a moment before turning back to their walk.

106

They walked through most of the day in the Treetop City. Pan would occasionally stop and talk to someone or introduce Jacob to another Orn. Jacob found everyone and everything very interesting. Each individual Orn looked as different as one human to the next, but each had pointy ears and wore the same style of clothes.

Pan showed Jacob the inside of some of the Orn dwellings that were in the trees. They were small round houses that had only three or four rooms depending on how big the family was. The furniture, made from wood, was handcrafted, but Jacob found that some of it grew out of the tree itself like the table in the council hall. He also found that upon entering each house, his nostrils were filled with the sweet smells of the wet wood.

While walking on the road, Pan stopped in an area that was wider than most of the roads and almost entirely unpopulated. Jacob walked right up to Pan before stopping to look around.

"What are we doing?"

"Jacob, have you ever used a sword before?"

"Uh, well, no," Jacob admitted.

"Then I think its time for your first lesson. Unsheathe your sword and face me."

Jacob felt sudden cold run over him that had nothing to do with the temperature in the forest. Pan really wanted him to fight him right there in the middle of the road. There was nothing to it but to do as Pan told him.

He reached his right hand to the hilt of the sword and pulled it from its sheath. The sword felt as naturally in his hand as a fishing pole would on a fine summer's day, and Jacob had done a lot of fishing in South Carolina. He felt suddenly that all this time it wasn't his finger he was missing but this sword, and now that he had it in his hand, his arm was complete again. He swung it through the air a couple of times to get the feel of it, and he turned back to face Pan.

A strange withered smile hung on Pan's lips. He looked at Jacob like someone who had just eaten their favorite piece of fruit that was juicy, ripe, and perfect on the tongue. He, in fact, thought that Jacob looked somehow complete, more himself, with the sword in his hand.

"Are you ready then?" Jacob asked Pan. Pan's eyes widened in surprise at the change that suddenly came over Jacob. To answer him, Pan attacked.

Pan's sword flew straight at Jacob's face; he parried the blow as if he were flicking a fly out of his face. The old days of fighting with sticks against Taylor came back to him, and he smiled at the thought of Taylor always getting angry with Jacob for being able to disarm him. Jacob was a natural swordsman.

Pan let his body go with the momentum of the sword and spun around, until his sword once again flew towards Jacob. Jacob blocked his offensive blow and brought around one of his own that almost connected with Pan. But before Pan could feel relief at having blocked that blow, Jacob had another coming and another and another. He was fighting with such fierceness that Pan could hardly keep up.

Finally, Jacob caught Pan's sword, spun his own around it, and sent Pan's flying. It landed on the edge of the road, sticking straight out of the wood.

Groups of Orns passing by had stopped to watch and all gasped at the outcome of the fight. Pan stood staring at Jacob with that same withered grin on his face, panting lightly. Jacob looked from Pan to the Orns surrounding them then down to his own hand that still held the sword outstretched toward Pan like he would kill him at the slightest movement.

"Did I do good?" he asked Pan.

Pan burst out laughing, and the surrounding Orns gave a round of applause. Small whispers of "hero", "prophecy", and "fall of the king" could be heard running through the din of the Orns. Finally, Pan told the onlookers to continue on their way, and he and Jacob sheathed their swords.

"Good work, Jacob," Pan said. "No one has disarmed me for quite some time."

"I don't know why, but when I had that sword in my arm, I felt full, like I could do anything," Jacob said.

"You're a natural. Training you will be easier than anyone I've ever trained before. Now we better get down to the ceremony."

"Aren't you going to tell me anything about the ceremony?" Jacob asked as they began to walk.

"There are a few things you should know. You saw the Odds collect Aural's body, right?"

He nodded.

"They are the death collectors. When someone dies, the Odds take them. But the Orns and the Elves don't die. If we are killed, the Odds collect our bodies, but if we choose to leave this world for good, we are taken by the Anjels."

"So the Anjels are the good guys?"

"Neither the Odds nor the Anjels have a side in all of this. The Anjels are pure beings, and I guess if I had to be sided with one or the other, I would take the Anjels. Like their name, the Odds are just kind of unusual. It is

109

rumored that they are faceless and once they take the bodies to In-Between, they rip the face off the corpse to wear as their own. Eventually, it rots off and they have to steal another one."

He shuddered before continuing on.

"Now the ceremony tonight is the farewell to an old Orn named Gallo. When an Orn chooses to bid farewell to the Goldwood Forest and Toratoga, it is a day of rejoicing for they will be in a happier place that is far better than here. Many of the older Orns as of late have been saying good-bye. This world is just too depressing lately.

"Gallo will be carried to the Colors Beyond, which is our eternal resting place. A place of beauty only seen by those who go forever. We have prophets who've seen it in their minds and have written it down, but somehow, writing just doesn't do it justice."

They'd reached the end of the road and were crowded in with a mass of Orns who were trying to get down the stairs to the ceremony. Jacob saw some baskets hanging just off the roads in the trees. Pan saw him looking and told him, "Those are normally only for emergencies. They are on a pulley system that allows you to jump in and get to the bottom in no time."

Jacob understood that it was s primitive elevator. They continued to stand in line for the stairs for the next fifteen minutes, and during that time, Alice found her way back to them. Her eyes were once again bright, and Jacob could tell that she'd spent most of the day mourning her sister.

They finally managed to get down the stairs, and they followed the mass of Orns to the ceremonial stage. A great mound of rocks sat under the city in the least tree populated area. Orns were already gathered around the rock formation, and Jacob could see that Galadawn stood talking to an Orn who looked twice his age.

The gathering Orns grew steadily quiet, waiting for the beginning of the ceremony. A few Orn children ran around, giggling as they played. All at once, the sunlight broke through the trees and landed squarely on Gallo and Galadawn standing on the rock's surface.

"My fellow Orns," Galadawn said at once, "we have come to give our fondest of farewells to our fellow Orn, Gallo."

At once applause burst forth from the surrounding crowd, and Jacob joined in enthusiastically. The joy in the place was contagious and inspiring. He looked to Alice who smiled brightly at him in spite of the tears in her eyes.

Galadawn raised his hands over the crowd, and the silence fell at once. "The time is upon us," he said. "Let us look to sky as we await the Anjel."

As one, the heads of all the Orns present bent back in anticipation of the coming Anjel. The sunlight continued to shine down through its hole in the treetops, and all at once, the sunlight wasn't the only thing coming through. A small shadow descended down through the branches. The Orns gasped and one shouted out, "I see it." A fever of excitement swept through the crowd.

The first thing Jacob noticed about the Anjel was the color. Living in the drab colorless existence from day to day, the first spot of color is the first warm day after a long hard winter. The body of the Anjel was entirely blue with white veins running through it. Great black, fleshy wings stretched out over a thin layer of bones curved out from the body to an arch high above its head then stretching down to below the knee before coming back to its torso. It was nothing like Jacob could have imagined.

When it landed, Jacob saw its features better, noticing first the large white eyeballs then the absolute lack of hair. The Anjel wore no clothes nor did it need to; there was no sex to be seen. He was even more surprised to see that there was no mouth, only a blanket of blue below the nose. Once the crowd quieted, the Anjel spoke without moving its mouth.

"Greetings," it said inside Jacob's head. Judging by the reaction of the Orns around him, everyone could hear the Anjel as it spoke into their minds. "Today, another of your people leaves you to enter the Colors Beyond."

The Anjel continued to speak, but suddenly, Jacob felt a great wave of curiosity crash over him. He closed his eyes and seized the moment. When he opened them, he once again saw the true essence of everything around him. He looked up to the rocks where the Anjel stood, but instead of seeing the body of the Anjel, there was only an oval of white light. He could see Gallo standing near it, so he knew it must be the Anjel. Another shape near Gallo must have been Galadawn, but his body was shriveled and his limbs stuck out at weird angles. Jacob didn't know what that meant and forced it from his mind.

He stood staring at the Anjel for just a moment when it spoke inside his head once again. "Come to me, Jacob," it said. Jacob, although startled, obeyed and walked up to the platform of rocks. Already, his abilities were strengthening. He held the moment like he was simply pulling a rubber band.

As soon as he neared the light, the Anjel spoke again. "Jacob, welcome to Toratoga," it said. "You have a difficult task ahead of you. Do you feel that you are ready for it?"

"Yes," Jacob responded, "At least, I think so."

"This task, I am afraid to say, will take everything from you."

Jacob hesitated before asking, "Do you mean I will die?"

"There is no need to fear Death. Some can even overcome it."

"Defeat Death?" Jacob asked, his forehead wrinkling with the thought. "Who are you?"

"My name is Elea; I am a messenger among the Anjels."

"Will the Anjels help us in the battle for Toratoga?"

"No, I'm afraid we cannot. But I will give you something to help you. Place your hand on the light, Jacob, and absorb the powers I give you." Jacob reached forward timidly and put his hand on the light. Just as when he absorbed the magic from the tree, he saw the inside of the Anjel's mind. But this magic was bright orange instead of the green from the trees.

Instantly, a bright tingling entered his hands and spread from there to his entire body. Jacob felt his limbs begin to shake as the tingling grew stronger and his palms burned. Finally, he let go of the light and bent forward, afraid that he would retch. At last, he controlled the tingling and was able to stand again.

"I warn you," Elea spoke again, "store this magic until you absolutely need it because you will, Jacob. Pull magic from trees when you need it, but save this for that one moment."

"But how will I know when that moment comes?" Jacob asked, feeling so very tired from the strain of absorbing the magic.

"You will know. You are stronger now than you were, but not yet as strong as you will be. You must release this moment before it kills you."

"Thank you," Jacob said. He turned to walk back to his place next to Alice, but his eyes were drawn suddenly to a great shadow in the crowd. A black mass, much the opposite of the Anjel's true form, stood out in the crowd, but there was one small difference between this and the Anjel: two bright red eyes could be seen looking out of the black mass. Jacob felt sure they were looking right at him.

A cold hand gripped his heart which began to hammer faster than it ever had. He tried to turn away from the black monster, but when he did, he stumbled and fell to the ground. The moment slipped from him and the colors were once again drained away, but Jacob was much too weak to notice. He fell into a deep, restless sleep, and Jacob Nine-Fingers knew no more of the ceremony.

Chapter 11

Peril

Many of the Orns in the crowd** at the ceremony that evening stood in silent shock as the little boy appeared out of the air on the rock platform next to the Anjel. A few let out screams of terror. The Anjel appeared not to notice the boy lying there beside him, but merely finished the speech and flew off through the trees with Gallo.

Galadawn stood there on the platform looking at the boy for only a moment before he spoke. "The ceremony is over," he said. "Gallo is gone. May you all rest well tonight." After that, he turned his back on the crowd and Jacob and walked off the platform.

Pan and Alice both rushed up to the platform where the crowd moved in closer to the unconscious boy. Two other Orn Warriors ran forward to assist their captain. Pan and Alice sat next to Jacob. Alice grabbed his hand while Pan spoke his name, trying to revive him.

"What happened?" Alice asked.

"He must've used magic to seize the moment," responded Pan. "He probably held it too long."

"This boy can use magic?" one of the Orn Warriors asked.

"Yes, Luminous," Pan said. "He has become very skilled in seizing the moment."

"You mean he can see the true essence of everything?" the Orn named Luminous asked.

"Of course," Pan replied, but as he said it, Jacob opened his eyes.

"Jacob?" Alice said. "Are you all right?"

Jacob looked from Pan to Alice and a small smile crawled over his mouth. "'M'all righ'," he murmured.

He tried to say more, but at that moment, Alice fell on him and embraced him in a great hug. He tried to return it, but his arms were still unsure of how to respond to the messages his brain sent them.

"Okay, Alice, let him breathe," Pan said.

Alice pushed herself off of Jacob's body, looking slightly embarrassed.

"Jacob, what happened?" Pan asked.

Jacob stared up at Pan for a minute before answering him. "I wanted to see the true essence of the Anjel, so I froze time," he said. "When I did, he invited me up to the platform."

"Wait," Pan interjected, "the Anjel could talk even though you'd seized the moment?"

"Yeah. So I came up here, and the Anjel told me some things," Jacob continued. "I guess I held the moment too long, because I fell over and that's all I remember." He couldn't bring himself to tell them about the great black monster he'd seen in the crowd.

"Do you think you can stand?" Pan asked.

Jacob nodded, and with the help of Pan, made it to his feet. The two Orn Warriors continued to stand by, waiting for an order from Pan.

"Ah, yes," Pan said once Jacob felt safe on his feet again, "Jacob, this is Luminous and Luthos. They will assist in your training."

Each of the Orns bowed to Jacob. "It is an honor," they said in unison.

"They are brothers," Pan said, looking at the two with a small grin.

Jacob nodded to each of them, but just as he was about to engage them in conversation, a loud horn blast broke through the air around them. The crowd had still not dispersed around them, but at the sound of the horn, the Orns broke into a mad rush to get to the stairs, to get to safety. Jacob looked to Pan with great round eyes.

"Go on, Jacob, get out of here," Pan shouted at him.

"I'm coming with you," Jacob replied.

"No, you're not. Go back with Alice. Hurry now."

But Jacob only stood staring at him. Alice grabbed his hand and tried to pull, but Jacob wouldn't budge. He held his gaze over Pan.

"I'm coming with you," he said again.

"Jacob," Alice said, "come on, let's go."

"Alice, go on. Get to safety. I'll see you soon," Jacob said, turning his attention to Alice, his voice softening. She nodded, assured by the determination in his voice. As she turned to run to the stairs, Jacob turned back to Pan.

"I'm not going to argue with you," Pan said.

"Good, because I am coming with you," Jacob responded.

Luthos and Luminous stared at Jacob, apparently amazed that someone would dare speak to their captain in such a way. Pan started to respond, but another Warrior leapt from a tree at that moment to land right beside Pan. He held a bow in his hand, but all his arrows were spent. He had a wild look in his eye and sweat moistened his already dark hair.

"Captain," the new Warrior said, "you must come."

"Regal, what is it?" Pan asked.

"Grebbles in the forest," Regal responded, struggling to catch his breath. "They're headed this way. Our defenses cannot hold them much longer."

"Grebbles? In the forest?"

Regal nodded.

"All right, Warriors, let's move out," Pan said, taking on a sheer determination Jacob hadn't seen in him before. "Jacob, stay close to me."

Pan turned to run back along the path he and Jacob had first taken to find the Treetop City. Jacob followed along, trying to keep up with his brisk pace. While they ran, they were joined by more and more Warriors, mostly Orns, but also a few men joined in. Jacob's heart raced at the thought of entering battle.

The group of Warriors only ran a short way before they met the Grebbles. Their blue skin almost seemed to shine in the shadows of the trees. Many of them held their own swords out in front of them while others had great spiked balls on chains as their weapons. The defense of the forest seemed to barely put a dent in the force of Grebbles.

The two armies met with a resounding clash that echoed around the huge trees. Jacob watched as one Warrior impaled a Grebble with his spear while another

Grebble took the head clean off of the Orn with his spiked ball. Soon blood flew up through the sky like a mass of flies. All that could be heard were the shouts of battle and the loud clang of swords.

Jacob dodged in and out of the constant foray of the Grebbles. He found Pan again after losing sight of him from the beginning of the battle. Pan fought two Grebbles fiercely, swinging his sword from one to the other, but each blow he dealt was parried by the Grebbles' swords. Jacob ran to his defense.

He swung his sword in a low arc that caught the unsuspecting Grebble below the knee. The Grebble let out a horrible yell as Jacob pulled his sword from the deep gash in the Grebble's leg. The Grebble's sword then came down to barely miss Jacob's head as he dove to his right. The Grebble, slower from its fresh wound, turned to find Jacob standing ready. Jacob's sword sunk into the belly of the monster up to the hilt, the point of the blade protruding from its back. The Grebble stared at Jacob and fell backwards as death overtook it.

Pan watched Jacob finish the beast, his own enemy vanquished. But before he could say anything, another horn blast broke through the sounds of battle. Pan's eyes grew huge as he realized the sound came from behind them, back toward the city

"Jacob, come on," he yelled.

"What is it?"

"Our entire fighting force is here. If something is attacking the city, it's completely defenseless."

Jacob understood and he took off after Pan who sprinted in the direction of the Treetop City to see what horrors awaited them there. A few of the Warriors, upon seeing their captain turn back, joined with Jacob and

Pan. When they reached the base of the city, the reason for the horn blast became obvious: the king's soldiers neared the group of Orns still gathered at the stair base.

Pan and his few Warriors ran forward to meet them. The men were not nearly as formidable opponents as the Grebbles were, but they vastly outnumbered the few Orns who turned back with Pan. Nevertheless, Pan led his army into a vicious attack on the men. Soon, the blood of the soldiers flew through the air. Several of the soldiers managed to run around the Orn defenses and continue running through the forest on the underside of the Treetop City.

Jacob saw the men go and ran after them. He felt brave; nothing could bring harm to him or to his new home. Soon, he saw the crowd of defenseless Orn women and children standing at the foot of the stairs waiting to ascend into the city. It amazed Jacob to see how many were still lingering at the bottom. The remaining Orns began to run as the soldiers neared them.

He turned back and screamed with every bit of strength he could muster, "PAN!" The captain of the Orn Warriors turned to Jacob and, looking past him, saw the soldiers gaining ground on the crowd. He grabbed his own horn and blew it, a shriller cry than that of the Warriors, in an attempt to rally his Warriors to protect their families. Then he ran. Jacob turned back toward the soldiers with Pan.

Orn Warriors joined them, hearing the blast from Pan's horn. In a matter of minutes, the Orns caught up with the soldiers who caught up with the crowd. The remaining soldiers, freed from battle after Pan's horn blast, came up behind the Orns, crushing the Warriors between two groups of fighting soldiers. The Orns fought hard but the blows coming from both sides were difficult to thwart, and many lay fallen across the bloody ground.

Jacob fought and killed three soldiers himself, but the day's battles began to wear him down at last. Despite his desire to help, his body could not continue on at such a vigorous pace. One soldier bore down on him and knocked his sword out of his tiring hands. Jacob fell to his knees and waited for the final blow that would kill him.

"I'll let the king take care of you," the soldier said in a gruff voice before his fist hit Jacob squarely in the jaw. The blow left Jacob dazed but still conscious. He spat blood out of his mouth to add to the already growing amount of blood on the ground of the forest.

The carnage about him seemed to stir a fire back inside of him. Bodies of Orn Warriors lay around him in heaps with the bodies of soldiers. He punched the soldier in front of him in the groin and felt something crunch beneath his knuckles. The soldier doubled over in pain and Jacob used the opportunity to pick up his fallen sword and shove it through the soldier's throat.

Then a piercing scream shattered the sounds of battle. The remaining Orns turned back to see soldiers running away from the crowd carrying something with them. Jacob thought that the Orns had at last won because all the soldiers seemed to be running that way, toward the beach.

"Jacob!" The yell came from his right. He stood and looked in that direction where Pan was running toward him.

"There you are," Pan said when he reached him. "Come on, we have to catch them."

"But why?" Jacob asked. His tongue felt thick and his head lighter than the air outside of it.

"They captured Orn women," Pan said.

The urgency in what Pan said to him seemed to pull him from his daze. Holding his sword tight in his hand, he took off with Pan after the soldiers.

They ran, never seeming to catch up with the soldiers who had a good lead on them. Occasionally, one would jump out of a hiding place to try and slow them down, but Pan in his ferocity, tore into them as easily as if they were merely figments of his imagination.

The weariness in Jacob doubled as he ran, but he continued, persevering through the worst of the pain. At long last, they emerged through the trees to land on the sand of the beach to find their own soldiers dying on the beach. The king's soldiers carrying the Orn women climbed into a small boat while the remaining soldiers hung back to fight off any pursuing Orns.

Again, Pan hacked into them with such vicious accuracy that their numbers fell as he gained ground on them. Jacob did his best to fight alongside his captain, but his arms were so tired he could barely do any damage. Huge oars emerged from the sides of the boat and sent it into the current of the sea. Pan yelled out in frustration at his failure to save the Orn women. The few soldiers remaining on the beach felt the full sting of Pan's wrath. Soon dead bodies of soldiers littered the beach and the spilled blood turned the sand of the beach black.

Pan ran for the sea, his legs splashing the water in high arches behind him. Jacob ran to catch him. "Wait, Pan," he said as grabbed hold of him. "Pan, it's too late. Can't you see?"

Pan stopped struggling and looked out at the sea and already the boat was only a spot on the horizon. His shoulders sagged down at the sight of it. "He's gone too far," he whispered. "We would never attack his women, his children. He goes too far."

Pan turned back toward Jacob and the beach. The fire had gone out of his eyes, and Jacob was almost sure he could see a trail of smoke in them.

"Are there any left alive?" Pan asked Jacob.

"Pan?"

"Are there any soldiers left?" Pan asked again looking at the beach. Jacob turned back to the beach just as Pan sprinted past him with amazing speed. He jumped and landed on a soldier who cried out. Jacob ran after to catch up to him.

"What did he want with them?" Pan asked in a low growl.

The soldier, though frightened, began to laugh. "You know what he's doing," he said, he sounded just as crazy as King Ro.

"What are his plans, maggot?" Pan asked again, this time using his fist to the man's gut to punctuate the question.

The soldier gasped, but didn't lose his grin. "Uruk Taki," the soldier said and resumed his bone chilling laugh.

"LIAR!" Pan shouted at him. "Don't lie to me."

"You know I'm not lying," the soldier responded.

Pan's fist flew hard and fast landing on the soldier's nose. Blood spurted forward from the busted cartilage, but the soldier didn't move anymore. Pan, breathing hard, stood slowly and turned back to Jacob.

"It's worse than I ever could have imagined," he said, barely looking at Jacob.

"What is it, Pan?" Jacob felt terrified. Pan was the bravest and strongest Orn he'd met in Toratoga, now he was seeing a scared and fragile child.

"The king, he's using the darkest weapon he possibly could," Pan said.

"What, Pan? What is it?"

"Black Magic," Pan said before turning away from Jacob, away from the beach, and walked back to the Treetop City.

Chapter 12

Uruk Taki

The sun once again ascended into the sky, forcing the shadows to jump around the feet of the weary travelers. Jacob tried to get Pan to stop for rest several times, but he was relentless. His need to get back to the Treetop City seemed almost as relentless as his need to rescue the Orn women, only less important. Jacob's body felt like a great boulder carried by his legs, his arms were sore from all the fighting, and each time he blinked his eyes it became harder and harder to open them again.

As they drew ever nearer to their destination, Jacob finally collapsed, his weariness overtaking him. It was a few minutes before Pan noticed that he was alone.

"Jacob?" he said, turning back to scan the area he'd just walked. He doubled back and found the child, curled into a small ball, sound asleep. A smile touched his lips as he remembered that Jacob was only a boy.

Pan stooped down and picked Jacob up off the ground and carried him the rest of the way to the Treetop City.

A great crowd of mourners stood at the base of the city much like the evening before while waiting for the Anjel. All of the fallen Warriors lay across the ground, awaiting their final ascent into the sky. As soon as Pan emerged from the wood around the crowd, Warriors rushed to his side.

"Captain," said Regal when he reached Pan's side, "we were afraid you'd fallen."

"We looked for your body among the dead," Luthos said, once he reached Pan, followed closely by his brother Luminous.

Luminous seemed to notice Jacob before the others. He looked from the boy to Pan and finally voiced his concern, "Sir, is the boy...?"

"No," Pan said without looking at any of them. His eyes held a distant stare where none but Pan seemed to be able to see. He walked past the Warriors, past the crowd, to stand between the living and the fallen. The crowd quieted instantly when he stood before them. He laid Jacob down, who barely stirred when he left the warmth of Pan's arms.

"This night, we've lost many," Pan said. "Our foes have entered our own territory, surprising us with their cunning and their ability to attack at our weakest moment. They too lost many, but their cost is nothing to their gain.

"Fellow Orns, the soldiers have stolen from our midst not just the lives of these Warriors, but six of our Orn women. I gave the best chase my legs would allow, but they managed their escape. I found one living soldier on the beach, and he confirmed my greatest fear: Uruk Taki."

A wail rode through the crowd like a tidal wave. Each Orn in the crowd felt the weight of what Pan said. The great cry even woke the weary Jacob from his sleep who leapt to his feet, afraid to find himself in battle once again.

"The king has invoked the use of Black Magic," Pan continued. "We must fight this. We will rally the Elves from the West, and we will fight!" The crowd silently nodded their agreement.

Jacob looked from the roaring crowd to Pan, and as soon as the crowd quieted, he asked Pan, "But what are the Uruk Taki?"

Pan gazed into Jacob's eyes, studying them. Finally, he spoke, but loud enough for the whole crowd to hear. "The Uruk Taki are an abomination, a creation, and among the most feared of all creatures in the histories of Toratoga. Their presence almost assuredly means the destruction of the Orns and the complete downfall of Toratoga."

"The histories?" Jacob asked after a moment of silence. "You mean, this has happened before?"

"Yes," Pan answered, "in the ancient writings of our people. The murder of King Anan by his most trusted ally, Hait. It is written that Hait killed the king in order to rule the country for himself, but he didn't know what would happen to the land. As it is now, Toratoga's color faded and evil dominated. The Orns and Elves and Humans rose up against him and the Grebbles, but not before he could create the Uruk Taki.

"He created six of the monsters. They are larger, swifter, and more cunning than most any Orn. Those six Uruk Taki wiped out a great number of our people before they could be stopped."

"How could they be stopped?" Jacob asked, feeling the excitement of some insight into how he could stop this king.

"Wait, Jacob, I will tell you in due time," Pan answered. "It is now time for the gathering of our fallen."

As soon as he said it, the crowd began to sing a woeful song that brought tears to Jacob's eyes almost immediately. The crowd swayed as one, mourning the loss of their loved ones, not only the soldiers, but the six women taken by the king. While they sang, Jacob sank slowly in with them, not wanting to see the Odds slide down from the sky to gather the slain. As he walked through the Orns, he found Alice. Her face was soaked with her tears, and she embraced Jacob when he reached her.

His weariness returned as the comfort and warmth of her embrace rolled over him. Her soft and tear-filled voice swam through his head, calming his every nerve until there was nothing left of him, until all he could do was sleep. Alice lowered him to the ground where he slept, undisturbed, and she watched as the blue lights fell through the trees, landing beside the fallen Warriors. The blue women appeared as soon as the lights made contact with the ground, and with one blink of the eye, they were floating off, back into the sky, with the Orn Warriors and the king's soldiers in their arms.

A still quiet fell over the crowd until one by one, each Orn turned back to the entrance of the city and climbed the spiraling stairs. Pan lifted Jacob and carried him into the city, taking him to Alice's house where he would stay while in Toratoga. His training would need to start, but Pan could see no need for beginning that day. Jacob had achieved more than most had expected of him.

Hours passed by, the afternoon sunlight fell lower and lower, slowly giving way to the evening. A steady sadness loomed over the Treetop City as the Orns went about their daily routines trying to suppress the feeling of loss that hung about their shoulders. Jacob slept, but images of the black monster he'd seen in the crowd during the ceremony haunted his dreams. The darkness of the monster enveloped him and pulled him into a hell where pain had no limits.

He awoke abruptly, leaping out of bed, prepared to fight the monster. His mouth fell open as he realized he was standing in a small round bedroom; the bed clothes were scattered from his recent bout with nightmares. Alice stood in the doorway smiling at the confused look on his face.

"Welcome to my home, Jacob," she said. Jacob turned to look at her and realized he was wearing only the underwear he'd worn into Toratoga. He grabbed the sheet off the floor and quickly wrapped it about his body. Alice laughed a beautiful sound like clinking crystal.

"Where are my clothes? My sword?" Jacob asked.

"Your clothes are here in my arms," and Jacob noticed for the first time the bundle of clothing she held. "I've cleaned them for you. They were covered in blood. Did you kill many?"

Flashes of the battle ran through Jacob's mind. He was amazed at the fact that he hadn't gotten killed by the soldiers, much less the Grebbles. "I did, but I don't know how," he said.

"Good. You truly are the hero I expected, Jacob Nine-fingers. No other youngling would be able to attack the Grebbles and live through it." Jacob felt his pride swell with her words. The fact that he'd killed Grebbles and lived through it did nothing for him, but the fact that he was living up to the expectations of Alice made him feel more complete somehow.

"This was Aural's room, by the way," Alice said after watching him for a moment. "We thought you deserved to stay here since it was you who saved her from the king's destruction."

"But she still died," Jacob said, unable to meet her eyes.

"But she died bravely, defending you." She threw him his clothes. "You better put these on; you have been summoned to council with the Tribesmen." She left the room, allowing him to dress in privacy.

He dressed slowly, his heart groaning at the thought of meeting with Galadawn again, the Orn he suspected was the traitor. But once he was dressed, there was nothing more he could do to delay his departure for the council hall. He said goodbye to Alice, thanking her for the clean clothes, and made his way out onto the streets of the Treetop City, his sword once more hooked to his hip.

Still reeling from his nightmare battle with the black monster, Jacob tried to clear his head as he walked. He walked right into a large Orn Warrior without even realizing it. He felt grateful when he saw that it was Pan.

"Jacob, are you all right?" he asked, his voice softer than usual.

"Yes, sir, I have a meeting with the Tribesmen," Jacob responded.

"Do you? Why was I not called also?"

"I don't know. Alice just woke me to tell me I was called."

"Maybe I should come with you."

"That would be excellent," Jacob said with true gratefulness.

Pan started to walk, but stopped as something caught his eye. Jacob's chin swelled slightly from the punch the soldier had delivered the night before. He tilted his head while looking at Jacob. It occurred to him that Jacob had not once mentioned the blow the soldier had given him, something most thirteen year-old boys wouldn't keep silent.

"Are you sure you're all right, Jacob?"

Jacob looked into Pan's eyes for only a second before dropping his gaze to the wooden road below his feet. *There's nothing left for it, little brother, just tell him.* Again Jacob was surprised to hear his brother throwing out a random comment after such a long silence.

"I have to tell you something, Pan. After I talked to the Anjel at the ceremony, I saw something terrible in the crowd. A great black mass with red eyes that looked right at me. It was one of the most frightening things I've ever seen."

Pan listened intently to Jacob and waited just a moment before responding. "I think you may have seen the traitor, Jacob."

"Do you really think the traitor was standing out in the crowd?" He thought of Galadawn standing on the platform with him.

"Yes, Jacob. In fact I'm almost sure that's what you saw. Someone who would betray their own kind is a worse evil than anything the king has committed so far. But just give that time." Pan's eyes seemed to fog over as his thoughts drifted out to the six Orn women who, at that moment, were probably being put to their use by the king.

"Is there no other explanation for it?"

"It must be the traitor. Tell me, what did the Anjel look like?"

"You've never seen the true essence of an Anjel?"

Pan shook his head. "Being that I was incapable of seizing the moment, I never saw the true essence of anything. I think you may be the first to have seen the true essence of an Anjel in all of Toratoga."

Jacob thought about it, recalling the memory of the Anjel in place of the memory of the monster. "He was basically the opposite of the monster in the crowd, a white mass with no definite shape."

Pan nodded his head. "That makes sense. The Anjel's are all good. There is no evil anywhere near them, so they would be completely white. The traitor, however, would have no good, not even a tiny shred of it. He's sold his soul to evil, so he is black. All black."

Jacob understood. That meant that the traitor was real, and that it wasn't Galadawn. "Do you think the traitor told the king about the ceremony?"

"I haven't thought of that. But yes, now that you ask, I do think that. That makes the traitor that much worse." Pan spat off the side of the road and walked away from Jacob. Jacob struggled to keep up.

"I saw Galadawn during the moment, as well."

"Uh huh. And what did he look like?"

Jacob got the feeling that Pan wasn't really listening, but he proceeded nonetheless. "His body was twisted and bent. I don't know what that means, but I thought I should tell you."

"What do you think it means?"

"I thought at first that he was the traitor, but now I don't know."

"You thought Galadawn was the traitor? I guess with the way he's treated you so far, I can see why you would think that. But his body being twisted is probably caused by the evil getting to him." He thought for a moment. "You should tell no else about this."

They walked through the city, up one sidewalk that led to the upper level, as Alice lived on the lower level. Eventually they stood, once again before the council hall.

"Are you ready?" Pan asked.

Jacob could only nod, but he managed. Pan looked to the Warrior who stood guarding the door to the hall. Ludlum stood at attention when Pan looked at him. "Sir," he said in a clear, loud voice, "only Jacob is allowed to enter the council hall for this council. I've been given strict instructions."

"Fine," Pan replied, "but I'm going in with him."

Ludlum looked away from the vacant spot he'd been staring at in the trees to Pan's face to see that his captain was serious. A small tremble seemed to shake through the guard's body, but he stepped out of the way to let Jacob and Pan through to the council hall.

The nine Tribesmen were once again sitting behind their table, waiting for Jacob to enter into their council. A murmur broke through them when they saw Pan escorting Jacob into the hall. Jacob walked calmly up to the accustomed spot where he'd already stood twice before, hoping that this time he would be treated decently.

"Pan, Captain of the Orn Warriors, you were not asked to come to this council," Galadawn said.

"Not only was I not asked to come, but Ludlum asked me not to come," Pan replied, a smile curling his lips.

"Never mind, Galadawn, we have urgent business," Elda said. Her voice, though small and fragile, commanded an audience, and everyone in the room listened. "Jacob, you are the only hope now."

"But," Jacob began, trying to find the confidence he had during both of the previous councils, "I thought I *was* the only hope to begin with."

"We were never very sure how much we would be able to accomplish without the use of magic, but many were still confident we would be able to defeat King Ro without any outside help.

"But now that the king has taken six of our women, we know his plans to create the Uruk Taki. And Jacob, I am afraid that the only way to defeat Black Magic is with Pure magic. The kind of magic that only one can achieve. And you've proven that that is you, my dear boy."

"You mean I have to single handedly fight the most feared monsters in the histories?"

"Yes, Jacob," Elda said quietly, and the already silent room grew quieter still.

"I don't understand, what is the big deal with these things?" Jacob said. "Why is this worse than anything else King Ro has done?"

"The process is simple. King Ro will burn the Orn women alive," Galadawn said. "Their bodies will become ash, a black grainy ash that, when combined with the living Grebbles, will create the Uruk Taki."

"How does he combine them?"

"He opens their skin to allow the ash contact with the blood stream of the Grebbles," Galadawn said. "The transformation is painful and terrible."

"But if he burns the women, how can they go with the Odds?"

"That, I am afraid, is the terrible part of the ordeal," Elda said. "The act of burning a body alive destroys every fragment of the person. There is nothing left of them to go on. They are simply gone."

"How am I supposed to defeat them?" Jacob asked. "How long before they are created?"

"We don't know how long," Galadawn said.

"As for how," Elda resumed the speech, "you must have one of our rings. The rings are made of the leaves from our trees and stones found in the Neverise Mountains to the north. The mountain dwelling Orns mine the stones. Combing the two with magic gives the ring a special power. Unfortunately, there are few left, and we've lost our contact with the Northern Orns.

"I loaned one to Alice so that she could enter you world to find you. She lost the ring when the Warriors took her prisoner. Now, we've run out of options. I'm afraid there is little we can do to get you a ring."

"But I can perform the magic," Jacob said.

"He's right," Pan said. "He could create a ring with his skill."

"But we have no stone for him," Galadawn said.

"Wait," Jacob said, thrusting his hand in his pocket to retrieve the broken ring his father had given him. "Is it possible to repair a broken ring?" He opened his hand and displayed the bent ring that had removed his finger.

"Where did you get that?" Galadawn hissed.

"It was my father's."

"How did it break?" Pan asked, now leaning in to get a closer look.

Jacob looked from Pan to the ring and closed his fist again. Then he told them the story of how he lost his finger. Elda smiled at the end of his tale.

"And he never told you where he got the ring?" she asked.

"No. I just always thought it was his school ring or something."

"Being that these rings are so rare, we would allow some people from your world to have a ring in order to go between the two worlds. Your father must have been a close friend to us. What was his name?"

"Ryan Kepler," Jacob said, feeling absurd for talking about someone who couldn't possibly know a thing about this world in which he now stood.

A murmur rolled through the Tribesmen and Pan looked curiously at Jacob. "I should have known," Galadawn said.

"Your father was a very great man," Elda said, ignoring Galadawn completely. "When he first entered our world twenty years ago, we'd begun a feud with our kinsmen, the Elves. Evil began to win in our hearts, and the colors started to fade.

"Your father helped us to end that war and restore peace to the Goldwood Forest. Because of that, he was welcome in Toratoga. So we gave him the ring."

Jacob couldn't believe her. His father would have told him something of this place if he'd been here. He was sure of it. But then again, he never once told him where he'd gotten the ring, so it was possible.

"Yes, Jacob," Elda continued, "you can repair a broken ring. But that is only if the stone is intact."

Jacob examined the shiny surface of the stone. Despite the tearing of the metal around it and loss of his finger in the process, the stone was intact, flawless. Excitement fell over Jacob in great waves.

"It's perfect," he said, refusing to take his gaze away from the stone.

"YES!" Pan exclaimed. A sense of relief filled the room, and finally Jacob tore his eyes from the stone. All the Tribesmen were smiling, even Galadawn, however small it was. "You can repair it, Jacob," Pan continued, "and King Ro will fall."

The rest of the Orns cheered along with Pan and the excitement in the room overwhelmed Jacob, but his heart still felt heavy at the thought of his dad visiting this world and never telling him about it.

"Pan, Jacob," Elda said, "you are dismissed. Pan, I expect you will show him the methods we have written on how to fix his ring?"

"Of course."

"Good. Now you better get your rest this evening. It will take every last bit of strength you have to repair the ring."

Jacob and Pan bowed to the Tribesmen and walked out of the council hall with a new purpose to pursue.

Chapter 13

The Ring Repaired

Jacob returned to bed that night in Alice's house but spent most of the night thinking of his dad and wondering what could have kept him from mentioning Toratoga to him. He thought to his last conversation with his mother and her confession of his dad talking in his sleep. Of course Jacob didn't think much about it at the time, only that it confirmed the existence of Toratoga. It didn't even occur to him to be shocked about the fact that he and Alice had the same ring.

He decided to talk to his brother about it, no matter how imaginary he was.

"Why do you think dad never told us about Toratoga?" he whispered into the night.

I don't know. Maybe something really bad happened while he was here.

This thought hadn't occurred to Jacob. "Do you think so?"

Sure. Remember that time we broke the window with that baseball and we didn't tell anyone about it for two hours?

"You broke the window, Taylor."

Yeah, but I was throwing the ball to you.

"You threw it way over my head. There was no way I could catch it."

Right.

"Taylor!" Jacob let his voice rise with the memory of the baseball incident. His brother had blamed him for not catching the ball.

Sorry. Anyway, that was something really bad and we didn't want to tell anyone about. Maybe something happened to Dad while he was here.

Jacob thought about it. Somehow, it made sense. "I'll ask Pan about it tomorrow. Maybe he knew Dad. I'm sure he was around when Dad came here."

Good thinking.

And the ease of that thought sent Jacob, at last, into a deep sleep. The monster stayed at bay in his dreams that night, but his Dad made several appearances. When the morning light crept through the tops of the trees, Jacob woke up to find Alice standing over him. At first he thought something might be wrong, but he saw the smile on her face and everything was all right.

"What a great way to wake up," he said with a slight yawn.

She gave a small giggle. "My parents have a meal prepared for you. And Pan is here. What happened at the meeting last night?"

Everyone had been in bed when he'd returned from the council hall, so he didn't have a chance to share the experience with Alice. He quickly told her what he had to do that day.

"I tried to stay up to wait for you, but I'm afraid I was just too tired. Yesterday was a big day."

"Yeah, it was."

"I better let you get dressed. Hurry so you can eat before you go."

He dressed quickly and rushed out of the room. Pan sat at a table with two other Orns who looked remarkably like Alice. Heaping piles of food were sitting on the table, so Jacob sat and helped himself. The conversation during the meal was light, but Pan hurried Jacob through it to get a start on their task that day. After Jacob had eaten his fill, the two thanked Alice's family for the food and went out to face the day.

"Jacob, I have someone I want you to meet before we get started," Pan said once they were out on the road. Jacob nodded and fell into place following Pan. His own thoughts still deep into his conversation with Make-Believe Taylor from the night before. He would wait until he and Pan worked on the ring before he asked about his father.

Pan led him farther to the west on the lower level of the city. They passed the underside of the council hall where the armory was, and on they went. They neared the very edges of the city when Pan led Jacob into a tree on the North side of the road. The door sealed shut behind him, but torches were burning brightly inside the tree.

When Jacob's eyes adjusted to the duller quality of light within the tree he could see that he and Pan were not the only ones there. A thin man with long hair stood facing them. At once Jacob could tell that he wasn't an

Orn. His tunic fit tighter, and his eyes were smaller. But his ears pointed up through his hair like the Orns. When Pan stood next to the man, Jacob saw that he was almost a foot shorter than the Orn.

"Jacob, this is Methindail. He is the captain of the Elvin army," Pan said. The Elf bowed to Jacob, and Jacob likewise bowed to the Elf.

"I am most pleased to meet you, Jacob Nine-fingers," Methindail said in a high-pitched raspy voice.

"I have told him about the Uruk Taki," Pan said, "and the Elves will join us on the battle field when that day comes."

"That is excellent news," Jacob said.

"No being in Toratoga should stand for such monstrosities," the Elf said.

"His armies are the best archers in our land," Pan said. "Their eyes are sharp, and their swords are swift. They are very formidable opponents."

"You speak kindly, Pan," Methindail said.

"He wanted to meet you," Pan said to Jacob. "They live far off to the west in their own village, but they too have felt the effects the evil King Ro has brought to our world.

"We have things we must attend to now, Methindail," Pan said turning back to the Elf.

"I look forward to standing on the battlefield with you," Jacob said, once more bowing to the Elf before walking out of the tree. Pan followed Jacob out. He reached into the branches very near the road and pulled out a thin grey rope.

"Grab onto this, Jacob, and swing," Pan said. Jacob looked up into the trees to see where the rope connected, but the branches were too thick.

141

"Where does it go?" he asked.

"I'll go first and show you," Pan said, pulling another grey rope out of the trees. He grabbed on and swung out into the shadow of the trees.

Jacob grabbed the rope and swung out into the darkness, the cold air rippling through his hair and clothes. At the end of his arch, he saw Pan standing on a wide branch, smiling brightly at him. He reached out a hand to help Jacob up onto the natural platform.

They repeated the swinging from several different branches in the trees. Ropes were hidden well within the trees. Jacob at least now understood how the Orns traveled so fast while following Pan through the forest.

At last, they reached the point that Pan aimed to reach, far to the Northwest of the Treetop City. Next to the branch they landed on was a tall thin pole hewn from the wood of one of the great trees. To Jacob it was simply a wooden fireman's pole only hundreds of feet high. The two hopped onto the pole and slid to the ground.

Near where they landed was the entrance to a clearing surrounded by large boulders that created a wall. Pan and Jacob entered the clearing through the entrance. As soon as Jacob entered the clearing, he felt a peace move through him. He looked up toward the sky and let the sunlight warm his cool face.

"This is where you will fix your ring, Jacob," Pan said. "None will bother you here, and as you've felt, this is the most peaceful area of the forest.

"You will need complete concentration for this. You have done extraordinary things so far, but this will be among the most difficult. You can bring magic into the circle with you, and you can release it into the circle. The power will hold here for your use when you are ready.

The amount of magic required to form the ring out of the leaves of the Goldwood forest is awesome.

"Here," he handed Jacob a large leaf from one of the trees above. "You can use this to repair the torn ring. All you must do is concentrate on it, pulling the magic you release into the circle through you and into the ring.

"I created this ring for your father. None know that but me and him."

"Is this where you created this ring?" Jacob asked.

Pan hesitated. "Yes," he answered, "but that was a long time ago."

"How well did you know my father?"

"The last time I saw your dad was right after your brother was born. He came to tell me and my wife, Eliza. He was so proud. I knew nothing of your existence"

"Your wife?"

"Yes. She left some time ago. She was sick and so full of pain. The sickness could not be healed, so the Anjel came to take her. It was the saddest day I've ever known. But I look forward to the day that I can meet her in the Colors Beyond."

"Why not just go now?"

"I cannot give up on my duty for my people. As much as I long to see her again, I could never leave here with so much undone."

Jacob felt he understood Pan's sadness for being unable to save the Orn women from the king's soldiers. Their husbands would never see them again. "And you never saw my dad again after that?"

"I only saw him once more. He returned to say goodbye only two or three years ago. That was the beginning of the evil here, although we didn't know it then. Having a son changed him somehow, and he felt that he needed to pay more attention to his wife and his family instead of spending so much time here."

"And he never brought my mom here with him?"

"No, she refused to believe him when he told her about Toratoga. She made him feel like such a fool that he never brought it up again. But he made more and more trips here. Until his son was born."

"Why do you think he gave me the ring instead of Taylor?"

"I can't say. Maybe he saw something in you that reminded him of himself."

"He never once mentioned where it came from. He never told me anything about Toratoga."

"He was trying to move on with his life, Jacob. You have to understand that he wanted to put that behind him."

Jacob nodded but felt there was something more. He and his father were very close, and he knew that his dad would have told him about this world. There had to be some major reason that would keep his dad silent all those years.

"Now, Jacob, you must start. The ring needs to be repaired, and it will take you some time to fix it. I will leave you now. Make for the city when you've finished. I will have the Warriors on the lookout for you."

Pan turned his back on Jacob and headed out of the circle. Jacob stood in the circle of stones for a moment trying to collect his thoughts. Everything he'd been told made some sense except for the fact that his father had failed to talk about the world at all.

"Why didn't he tell me?" Jacob said out loud as soon as his thoughts threatened to overtake his mind completely.

Something must have kept him from it.

Jacob was never more grateful for the sound of his brother's voice, no matter how imaginary it was. "But what could it have possibly been?"

Didn't his brother die about the same time he gave you the ring?

Jacob thought back. There'd been no funeral, only a memorial service. His uncle's body had been lost. His dad told him that he'd always imagined his uncle being a pirate lost out at sea, although Jacob had never met the man. When they left the church where they had the memorial service, Ryan, Jacob's dad, pulled the silver ring from his pocket and gave it to Jacob.

"Yes, he gave it to me right after Uncle Gail's memorial service."

How long did you have the ring before you lost your finger?

"I don't know, just a year, I think. Maybe more. And it was only a couple months after that that mom and dad split and I moved to Oklahoma." The memory of it still stung.

So it must have been Uncle Gail's death that forced him to give up the ring.

"Yeah, and when the ring broke, he wasn't the same anymore, so Mom decided to leave him." At that thought Jacob had an immediate need to repair the ring. He felt that if he repaired the ring he would somehow repair his parent's marriage. Nothing in the world made him as happy as that thought.

He ran out of the circle and looked about the forest floor. Not far from the circle of stones, he found a flat black stone with a light sheen to it. He lifted the stone out of its embedded spot in the earth and carried it to the center of the circle, again noticing the sense of peace that filled him when he entered the ring of stones.

He pulled the ring from his pocket and, placing it on the leaf Pan had given him, laid the two on the stone. Once more he rushed out of the circle to gather magic. He put his hand on a tree and felt the tingling spread through his arm. The forest was already beginning to trust him.

He ran back into the circle and released the magic, careful not to release the magic the Anjel had given him. He pictured in his mind the magic from the Anjel to be a bright orange color and the magic from the tree to be green. He could easily access them at different times by color coding them.

The magic drifted out of the stub he had remaining of his right index finger. The tingle boiled down through his arm as the magic left his body. He felt his hair begin to rise with the magic in the air around him. As soon as he depleted it, he ran back out of the circle to repeat the process.

He gathered magic from all of the surrounding trees, and every time he entered the circle, the air felt lighter and there was a definite tingle in the air that reminded him of the tingle that spread through his arm as he gathered the magic. He gathered magic from forty trees, making several trips to some. At last he took one last pull from a great tree and walked back into the circle.

The sun neared its peak as the noon hour arrived. The grey sunlight fell into the clearing, but turned bright yellow when filtered through the magic in the air of the circle.

Jacob stepped into the circle and blinked back the amazing quality of yellow sunlight. His feet left the ground as he entered the circle, and he hovered above the now green grass to where the black stone floated in the center; the ring and leaf now silver, floated above it.

When he reached the stone, he put out his right hand and covered the ring and leaf, pushing them back on top of the stone. He closed his eyes to block out all distractions around him; he needed complete concentration to complete this. He opened his mouth and breathed deeply, feeling the magic enter his body through his lungs. The magic flowed through his body, flowing through his veins along with his oxygen. He sucked in air once more, and he let the magic flow.

The magic shot like fire through the palm of his hand to land on the ring under his hand. He bent his will upon forming the ring the way it once was, when he still had ten fingers. He continued to pull in air and magic. The magic flowed through him right into the ring. Slowly, he sank back into the ground, the sunlight once more turned grey, and the grass faded back to black.

The magic flowed and flowed, and Jacob felt that his limbs may just fall off his body from the amount of tingling that wove through them. At last, he depleted the last of the magic in the air around him. The tingling in his arms subsided, and he opened his eyes. He removed his hand from the ring and gazed down at it.

Nothing was left of the stone but a pile of black dust. Sitting on top of that black dust was the ring. The ring itself remained silver and the stone green, and it was once again complete. A perfect circle. Jacob lifted the ring from the dust and felt the tingle shoot through his fingertips at the touch. He slipped the ring onto the stub of his index finger, and at once, the stone shone a bright green. Magic flowed through the ring, and Jacob felt more powerful than ever before having the ring on his finger.

He stood and walked out of the circle, back to the Treetop City.

Chapter 14

Restoring Hope

Jacob **walked back** to the Treetop City slowly. Every step of the way he felt different. The experience in the circle changed him, but he couldn't understand how. He walked with his head heavy with thought. He wanted to understand how the magic had affected him, but he couldn't. He wondered if he'd used too much magic when attempting to repair the ring. He looked down at the ring on his hand. The stone was still bright green set in beautiful silver. Jacob couldn't believe he had color.

Jacob could see the Treetop City high up in the trees when he heard a whistle far above him. He looked in that direction, but could make nothing out. He heard an answering whistle far off in front of him and knew that it wouldn't be long before Pan came out to meet him. He stopped walking and sat on a large tree root jutting out of the ground. After about five minutes, Pan came walking out of the trees directly in front of Jacob. His eyes fell on Jacob and he immediately stopped walking.

"Jacob?" he asked.

"I was only gone for a little while, Pan, surely you can recognize me," Jacob said, but even as he said it, he knew that he looked somehow different.

"You...you just look so much...older," Pan managed. "And your eyes, they're green. Really green."

"What? Come on, Pan, there's no need to joke."

"I'm not. Your eyes are green and you hair is long."

Jacob reached his hand up and felt his hair that fell down to his shoulders. "But that's not possible. My hair was barely an inch long this morning." Jacob stood, looking outraged at Pan.

"Jacob, it is possible. You used magic, anything is possible with magic. And it wasn't this morning."

"Yes, it was this morning. You left me right before noon."

"No, Jacob, I left you three days ago just before noon. The forging of the ring usually takes seven days, I was surprised to hear that you were back already. The days go by in what seems like only a few moments. Because of all of the magic in the air when you enter that circle, things change, rules bend and break, so you can never predict what will happen."

Pan hesitated a moment as if pondering that circle of magic, remembering how he felt there and finally asked, "Can I see the ring?"

Jacob held his hand out, the silver ring hugging the flesh of his stump, and for a moment he thought he saw the ghost of his finger with a slight green tinge to it. The vision was gone as soon as it appeared, but he was almost sure he saw it.

"It's beautiful, Jacob," Pan said, leaning over the freshly repaired ring. "You've done better than what it was in the first place."

"No, I think it was better before," Jacob said.

"But you returned its color to it, which reminds me, you have to come with me."

"What is it?"

"You'll see. It's only a small distance from here."

Pan set off at a brisk pace, and Jacob found that he could easily keep up. They walked south for about ten minutes, dodging through the trees until Pan stopped abruptly after rounding a small cluster of trees. Jacob saw a small crowd of Orns as soon as he came around the trees. In the midst of the Orns was a golden tree with silver leaves. Some of the Orns standing around it had tears in their eyes. Others sat looking up at the tree in awe. When they noticed Jacob standing near them, they cheered and several gave him hugs or pats on the back.

"These have been popping up in all kinds of places throughout the forest for the last few days," Pan told him. "Ever since I left you in the circle, color has been making its way back into the forest. Random trees like this one have color. And not just the trees. Though none of the trees have come back from the desert, it's been so long since we've seen color that we now have reason to celebrate. You did this, Jacob."

Jacob's eyes darted from Pan to the tree, and he walked, through the people, up to the tree. He reached out his right hand and felt the rough bark. Instantly, the stone of his ring began to glow, and the magic began to flow into his body once more, but the tree retained its color.

"Do you feel it?" he asked as he turned back to the Orns. "It's alive. Can you feel it?"

"Your eyes," one Orn whispered. "They're green."

Jacob looked at her. "They've always been green," he said, and he reached out his missing index finger and touched her with the stub. He released the magic into her and watched her eyes turn blue. "And now yours are blue."

He gave her a smile but slipped away as all the other Orns gathered around her to see the transformation of her eyes. He walked back to Pan.

"We should discuss making a journey," he said to Pan.

Pan's mouth hung open. "You've changed her eyes. You've given her color," he managed to say.

"Yeah," Jacob said, smiling at the Orn. "Let's go back to the city. I'd like to see Alice, and then we should talk."

Pan agreed and the two set off for the Treetop City. After they'd climbed the stairs, Jacob found himself smothered in a great hug. Alice had been waiting his return ever since she'd watched Pan leave the city to retrieve him.

"You're back!" she said too loudly in his ear.

"Yes," he said with a smile, enjoying the embrace. Despite the difference in his looks, she still knew him, and that brought him joy. "Was it really three days?"

"Yes! I couldn't believe how long it took, but Pan kept assuring me you were all right. He went out daily to check on you."

Jacob broke the embrace and found Pan standing behind him. Pan averted his eyes from the green ones of Jacob. "You checked up on me?" Jacob asked.

"Of course," Pan replied, looking full into the green eyes to answer the question. "I couldn't let anything happen to our hero, could I?"

"I guess not," Jacob said, turning his attention back to Alice. She gasped when she looked into his eyes.

"Jacob, your eyes, your hair, everything is so different," she whispered, her eyes taking in everything all at once.

"Yes, I know," he said, and reached out with his right hand and touched her forehead with the stub of his finger. Again, he felt some of the magic he'd absorbed from the tree flow into Alice. She smiled at the sensation she felt.

"What happened?" she asked when Jacob took his hand away.

"Do you have a mirror?" he asked.

"Yes, this way."

And she led him down a sidewalk that went off the main road through the trees. Pan followed behind the two. The sidewalk stopped on the top of a small tree so that a platform was created. The top of the tree came through the sidewalk but had been turned into a three-foot tall basin, almost like a birdbath out of wood. Looking at it, Jacob thought that it had been created by a gifted wood turner.

When they neared it, Jacob could see that it was filled to the brim with water, and it created a nice mirror. Alice stepped up to it and looked into her once more purple eyes that reflected back at her. She gasped lightly and a tear formed in the corner of her eye only to fall off into the still surface of the water. The water rippled for a moment before stilling again.

"Jacob, thank you," she whispered, not taking her eyes off of her reflection.

He smiled. "I couldn't stand to not see your beautiful eyes anymore."

"You should have a look at yourself," Pan said from behind. Jacob nearly jumped, forgetting for the moment that he and Alice were not alone.

He walked up to the basin to stand next to Alice and peered into the surface. There he saw a glimmer of who he last saw in a mirror. The Jacob now standing before him, while colorless, had long wavy hair, and small wrinkles around his eyes. He'd aged in those three days. Maybe not in years, but his body looked older, felt older, and the realization fell upon him that this was his destiny. He was meant to save these people. It only made sense that his dad would give him the ring, now that he thought about it. It made sense that he and Taylor spent hours having sword fights. Somehow, everything prepared him to come to Toratoga and save this world. And thinking of that, he felt helpless. His hope fleeted from him, and all he wanted was his mother.

Finally, he tore his eyes off of the green eyes reflected in the pool. He looked to Alice who stood watching him. "That's my reflection," he said, "but that's not me."

Alice didn't know what to say, but stood looking at him. Something about the tone of his voice scared her.

"Of course that's you, Jacob Nine-fingers," Pan said.

"And that's not my name," he whispered. "I'm Jacob Kepler. I'm only thirteen. I'm only a boy. Can't you see that?" Tears formed, magnifying the green in his eyes.

"No, Jacob, you're not only a boy," Pan said. Alice watched silently. "The magic is in you. You're greater now than you've ever been and ever would have been had you not come here. You're better than me, Jacob, and you're greater than King Ro. You were meant to save us."

"But what if I can't? Have you thought of that? What if I can't save you?"

Pan didn't have the words to respond to that. Jacob felt his hope fall with his lack of response. He'd felt that Pan could restore come confidence but he could see he was mistaken.

"But, Jacob, you're here," Alice said, finding her voice. "You came because you had the same confidence."

"It was easy when I lived in Oklahoma and none of this seemed real."

"But here you are, and you can see that this is real. You've done things nobody else can do. You have to defeat King Ro. I believe in you. If I hadn't, I wouldn't have risked everything to come get you."

"But you didn't know me before that. You were only going on what some old woman told you. This *is* real, Alice, and I'm scared. There's a huge chance that I can't save this world."

"You're right, this is real. And it's my home, the only home I have. If King Ro continues on, we'll be slaves to his cruelty. When that happens, we'll look forward to the day that Toratoga destroys itself and we're no more."

Her body shook with the emotion pouring through, and to Jacob, it was more powerful than the magic that discharged through his body in the circle. His heart broke watching her. He'd never considered girls before, he'd been too young. They were strange in their intoxicating ways; the way they could make boys act like morons to get their attention, and as soon as they got it, the girls simply walked away, leaving the boy feeling stupid and alone.

No, Jacob stayed far away from that, at least until he understood it better. But Alice wasn't like those girls at home. She never expected him to stand on his head or run head first into a tree just for her sheer enjoyment.

There was something else there, and he could feel it when she looked at him, when she hugged him. Affection rose up inside of Jacob, and all at once, he felt he could stop King Ro; he could save the world, as long as he had that affection from her.

He stepped up to her, wrapping his arms around her to still her shaking. She looked into his eyes, the green color reflecting her purple and felt his heart slamming into her own chest as if it were her own heart trying to get back in. He inched forward, not letting the fear sweep him away again.

His lips met hers; they sank into each other, feeling complete at last. Their lips tingled, and Jacob's ring shone a brighter green than it had yet. At last, every stupid thing he'd ever seen a boy do to get the attention of a girl made sense to him. He'd walk on hot coals for Alice, swim across an ocean, or face King Ro head on in a battle to the death. All because of one kiss.

When their lips broke apart, Jacob whispered, "I'm sorry."

"Forget it," she whispered back. "Just kiss me again, and we'll call it even."

And once more, their lips met.

Chapter 15

A Journey to the South

"**Are you two finished yet?**" Pan asked. Jacob and Alice jumped apart, remembering suddenly that Pan stood there with them. "I mean, I'm as excited as anyone will be about the possibilities of young love, but we've got a war to prepare for."

The two smiled sheepishly at Pan and reluctantly walked away from the basin.

"What was it you wanted to talk to me about?" Pan asked Jacob as they walked back up the sidewalk. Jacob's eyes lit up; he'd forgotten all about that in the excitement that followed arriving at the city. They stopped when they reached the road to talk.

"We should go to the south," he responded, watching Pan carefully for his response.

Pan's eyes narrowed slightly but showed no other reaction. "Why?" he asked.

"For one, I think we need to spy out the king. We need to know if he's started the process of creating the

Uruk Taki. We may need to rush into battle before he's finished creating them.

"And second, I would like to check up on William and his family. They showed me hospitality, and I would like to make sure they are all right."

"Hospitality? Aren't they the ones that turned you in?" Alice asked.

"Yes, but only because they had to. I went with William without any fight even though I knew where he was taking me. They only did it because they had to."

"So you want to go sneaking into two different towns to satisfy your curiosity?" Pan asked.

"Yes. But also because it will allow us the upper hand. Do you have horses?"

"Yes, we have a few, but Jacob this is madness."

"Is it, Pan? I think that it's madness to put all of your faith into a thirteen year-old boy. But what do I know?"

"All right, point taken, but do you really think we can sneak into two towns filled with the king's soldiers undetected?"

"William's town will be easy. The wall is small and they have only one guard at the gate. I just need to know that he's all right.

"The king's city will be tremendously difficult, but with a little magic, we should be able to get in without anyone knowing we're there."

"When should we go?"

"Now. Or at least as soon as possible."

"I agree. We should head out as soon as we have the horses loaded," Alice said.

Jacob turned to her, surprised by her comments. "You're not going with us," he said.

"And why not, Jacob?" she asked, the color rising in her cheeks.

"This will be very dangerous, Alice. If Pan and I go alone, it will be much easier to disguise ourselves. If there are three of us, I don't know if I will be able to do it."

"Sure you will," Pan said, surprising Jacob again.

"What?" he said, turning to Pan. "You want her to go?"

"Why not? We could use the extra horse for supplies, and she is pretty skilled with a sword, should it come to that." Alice's eyes brightened at Pan's words.

Jacob looked from Pan to Alice and at last he said, "Okay. Come with us, but you better not get yourself hurt."

"The same goes for you, Jacob," she said, the fire dancing back into her eyes.

They spent the rest of that day and early evening preparing for the journey that would start the next morning. They worked without anyone taking notice. Jacob couldn't help but think the traitor would find out what they were doing and warn the king. He suppressed that fear as the darkness fell once more onto the city and no one watched them as far as he could tell.

By nightfall, they had three horses prepared for the long journey and they had their supplies ready to throw over the horses. They agreed to meet at sunrise the next morning to head out. Pan bade Jacob and Alice goodnight as they headed down to the lower part of the city to Alice's house. As they walked, Alice reached out and grabbed Jacob's hand in her own and he felt his heart swell.

They stopped on the sidewalk that led to Alice's house and they kissed once more. The night breeze blew around them, chilling their skin lightly; Alice suppressed a shiver as she experienced another kiss with Jacob. When their lips parted, Jacob looked into Alice's eyes, feeling very much like an adult for the moment. He stared into her beautiful eyes and plucked up the courage to express his feelings.

"Alice, I've never..."

"I know," she interrupted. "Neither have I."

He smiled at her. "Would you consider not going tomorrow?"

Her eyes dropped from his. She felt his caring and knew instantly why he would want her to stay; she wanted him to stay, as well, to avoid the dangers of the journey.

"I can't, Jacob," she whispered, "I have to go with you. To keep you safe."

He had to smile at that. "Okay," he said.

"Okay? Can we drop it now and get some sleep?"

"Yeah, sure."

They walked the rest of the sidewalk to Alice's house and only separated to go to bed. Jacob hit the bed with the memory of Alice's lips on his until the sleep took control of his mind.

Jacob had to wake up Alice the next morning. He walked into her room and found her clutching her pillow tight with a smile on her face. The peace she had in her mind would leave her as they faced the dangers of their journey. He shook her gently and her eyes opened wide.

"Hi," he said. She smiled at him and pulled him down into a wonderful kiss that almost melted their lips with the passion of it.

"Good morning," she whispered when their lips parted briefly.

He finally broke from the kiss and left the room to allow her to dress. The house was quiet since most Orns didn't get up before the sun as Jacob had that day. He only had to wait a moment before Alice was with him and they headed down to the ground where the horses waited.

They found Pan waiting for them, already loading the horses with the pack of their supplies.

"Good morning, Pan," Jacob said when they saw him.

"We were watched last night," Pan said, not breaking from his work.

"We were?" Jacob asked, his heart suddenly leaping into overdrive.

"Yes," Pan replied and pointed to a tree not far away. Jacob saw nothing strange until he noticed the small branches lying at the foot of the tree.

"Was someone standing in the tree?" Alice asked as Jacob went to investigate the branches. They had obviously been cut clean from the tree.

"Someone stood up there, but apparently weren't able to see us. They had to cut away the excess branches to be able to see us."

"Should we call it off?" Jacob asked, rejoining them.

Pan, surprised by Jacob's comment, said, "I thought you knew we were facing dangers. Why would you want to call it off because one of our own people saw us planning?"

"You know why, Pan. It could have been the traitor."

"There's a traitor?" Alice asked with a gasp.

"Yes," Jacob said and quickly filled her in on everything they knew about the traitor. Then to Pan he said, "Have you not thought of that?"

"Of course I have, but we are facing many dangers, Jacob, this one does not concern me."

"What if he warns the king of our coming?"

"How could he do it so fast? He would have to be able to fly there to beat us."

Jacob understood his reasoning and reluctantly agreed to continue with their plans. They loaded their horses and set off through the Goldwood Forest. When the magic still existed, the Orn magicians had moved the trees around to create a path that led out of the forest to South, so that the horses could avoid the lake and have a sure footing through the trees. To avoid enemies finding the path, it curved in all directions, so only the Orns could find it.

The path amazed Jacob who could see the signs of the magic used to create the path. Destroying the trees would not have been allowed, so they simply pushed them out of the way using magic.

Jacob, Pan, and Alice rode along the path at a quick pace, and by the time they reached the grey dessert at the forest's edge, the sun had nearly finished its descent.

"Which should we visit first, Jacob?" Pan asked as they studied the horizon.

"I want to save the king for last," Jacob said. "Let's go see William."

"You better get some magic before we cross the desert," Pan said. "You'll not find any in this wasteland."

"Why not?"

162

"This desert has not always been here. The trees were destroyed by evil and all that's left is this grey sand. The trees are gone, so the magic is gone."

Jacob felt sadness at the thought of all those trees crumbling into sand. He remembered when King Ro murdered Aural that the trees nearest to her collapsed. He turned back to the trees he'd just left and refilled his magic supply, still hoarding the Anjel's magic until the time was right.

When he was finished, Pan said, "Right, let's roll along the forest line to be safe, and once we're even with Smoketown then we'll head back to the south."

"Is that the name of the town where William's family lives?" Jacob replied.

"Based on your description, that has to be it."

"Okay, let's get going."

They traveled on well into the night, feeling the cold wind of the desert like Jacob did his first night in Toratoga. Eventually, he became too tired to ride any longer and the three dismounted, still close to the forest, and slept for the night. They set off once more the next morning before sunrise.

"We should reach the town this evening," Pan told Alice and Jacob.

"Should we begin our plan tonight then?" Jacob asked.

"I think so. With the cover of darkness on our side, I think we would be fools to wait until the morning."

They rode through the entire day. Jacob's legs ached from the constant riding he wasn't used to. When the last of the sun's rays began to blink out, Jacob could just make out the walls of the town off to his right and to his left, he saw the group of trees where William found him on that first night.

They rode toward the wall of the town.

They left their horses tied up some forty yards away from the edge of Smoketown and headed to the wall. They pulled the hoods of their Orn cloaks up around their heads and walked around to the front gate.

"What are we going to do?" Pan whispered.

On a spur of inspiration, Jacob put the stub of his finger up to his throat and released a small amount of magic. He walked up to the gate and knocked.

He heard the familiar voice speak up at once. "What's the password?"

"Ham, shut your mouth, its jus' me William," Jacob responded, his voice sounding just like the soldier he meant to see.

"William? But how did you get out?"

Pan raised his eyebrows when Jacob looked back him. "I jus' got out, ya nitwit, now let me in," he said.

To Jacob's extreme relief, the gate latches went back and slowly, the gate opened. His hope fell a little when he saw four guards standing at the gate's entrance.

"You're not William," the short guard Jacob recognized as Ham said. "You're dressed as Orns. You're Orns!"

The four guards rushed the three weary travelers. They pulled their swords from their sheaths and fought but didn't kill any of the soldiers. Jacob decided on their way that they should avoid killing at all costs. Instead, Pan, Alice, and Jacob just managed to knock out the guards. They hid the bodies and passed through the gate.

They made it into Smoketown.

Chapter 16

A Traitor and a Hero

They walked cautiously through the streets. Every step they took screamed in Jacob's mind. He knew they would be caught and killed, and it would be his fault. They passed the pub, watching it for any signs of soldiers leaving for the evening. The clear streets felt odd to Jacob, but that thought fell from his mind when he spotted William's house.

"There it is," he whispered to Pan and Alice.

They crept up to the house, staying in the shadows, and Jacob knocked on the wooden door. The low drum of it resonated through Jacob as he attempted calm himself. He heard footsteps within and at long last, the door opened. There stood Lorrie in the doorway, looking at her late night guests.

"My lady," Jacob whispered with a bow, "could we come in?"

"Who're you and what do you want from me?" she asked, clearly frightened.

"I assure you we mean no harm to you or your family."

"Then why do you come in these hooded cloaks in the dark of the night?"

Jacob lifted his hood off of his head in response. She studied him for a moment in the gray firelight.

At last she said, "I know your face, but not why. Who are you?"

In answer to her question, he put his right hand out to her. Her eyes fell to the missing finger and flew back to his face and grew twice as big in the process.

"We did what we had to do. Honest. There was no other way to it." Her voice began to tremble with each word she managed to spit out.

"I am not here to harm you, Lorrie. I came only to check on your family and help you in any way I can."

Her fears sank away and she calmed with the ease of Jacob's voice. "All right, come in."

The three stepped over the threshold and walked into the small house. Everything in the house was just as it had been on the night Jacob first entered it. That night seemed like years before to him now. He wondered if Harold and Francis could continue to sleep with the noise of visitors.

"Where is William?" Jacob asked, looking about the room expectantly.

"He's gone. They've taken him."

"They've taken him? Where?"

"I'm not completely sure where. I think he may still be in town, but they might have moved him already."

"Why did they take him?"

"Well, because of you. You made the king look like a fool, chasing after a small boy in the middle of the city

166

and coming back empty handed. He had to punish someone and that fell to the man that turned you in. He's been gone a few days now, but one of our friends said he'd be held here until the king came to dispose of him." She broke down crying, unable to bear the thought of losing her husband.

Jacob turned to Alice and Pan. "What do you think?" he asked them.

"Looks like we're going on a rescue mission," Pan said.

Alice nodded. "This is why we came, right?"

"Right," said Jacob, and to Lorrie said, "Where exactly is he being held?"

Lorrie's tears cleared. "There's a small prison on the west end of town. I can't be sure, but I think that's where he is. Do you think you can save him?"

"Yes, I believe we can."

"But what will happen to us then? We can't stay here with a fugitive."

"No, you can't," Pan said, lowering his hood to reveal his pointed ears and long hair.

"You're an Orn." Wonder filled her as her eyes fixed on Pan.

"I am Pan, captain of the Orn Warriors. We have been hiding soldiers and their families from the king ever since this all broke out. We could easily find a place for your family."

Overcome with emotion, Lorrie began to cry once more.

"We'll have to hurry," Jacob said. "Lorrie, you need to get all the essentials you'll need from you house. Don't worry about clothes or food. Get your sons and anything you can't live without. We will go and rescue your husband."

Pan and Alice seemed determined, yet unfazed by this new turn of events. They walked out of the house a few minutes later with a few ideas on how to get William out of the prison. They all agreed that it should be as quiet as possible. They snuck through the alleys of the town to the west where Lorrie told them they would find the prison.

"This is so strange," Pan whispered as they snuck through the dark.

"What is?" Jacob asked.

"That there are no soldiers after us yet. I thought that our stunt at the gate wouldn't go unnoticed this long."

"Let's just get William out then we can worry about it."

They walked the rest of the way in silence, but a creeping fear started up Jacob's spine. It was too quiet on the streets of the town. It was late, and perhaps most of the town was asleep, but during such a dangerous time, there should be soldiers out walking around. He tried to push the thoughts from his mind, but it seemed that some evil lurked in the dark around them.

At last, they reached a small round building with no windows. One small door faced the main road, unguarded. Something about that felt strange to Jacob as the three went up to the door.

"Should we just walk right in?" Jacob reached for the door.

"This feels so strange," Alice said.

"I agree, but what choice do we have?" Pan said.

Jacob nodded and pushed on the door. To his relief, it wouldn't budge.

"It's locked."

"That makes me feel a little better, but what do we do now?" Pan asked.

Jacob put his right hand up to the door and pushed again, this time using magic to assist him. The door broke to pieces and Jacob stepped through the opening.

The inside of the building was one room. Three separate cells lined the walls and the middle contained the only prisoner. He jumped to his feet when the door broke, afraid that the king had come at last. Confusion replaced fear when he saw the three cloaked figures walk into the room.

"William?" Jacob asked. "Are you all right?"

"Who's there?" William asked.

"Jacob. Jacob Nine-fingers."

"Jacob? You're alive?"

"Yes, William. I'm here to save you."

"But 'ow did ya know I was in trouble?"

"I didn't. I just wanted to come here to see you and your family. I'm sure I would have died out there without your help that night."

"But I took ya ta the king."

"Only because you had to."

"Yeah and look where it got me."

"Jacob, we should hurry," Pan said. "You can catch up later."

"How're ya gonna get me outta here?"

"Let me worry about that."

Jacob extended his right hand and pulled out the last bit of magic from the tree. Despite his strength growing, he noticed that it still took a great deal of magic

169

to do the simplest things. A green jet of light shot out from the stub of his index finger and connected with the bars on the cell door. Instantly, they disappeared. The light vanished, leaving an image burned into the eyes of everyone in the room, and Jacob collapsed.

William came out of the cell. "Wha' happened?"

Alice screamed and rushed to Jacob, holding him in her arms.

"That was a difficult bit of magic he just did," Pan said, staring down at the boy. "I'm surprised he's still alive. But I guess this isn't the first time he's surprised me."

"Jacob?" Alice ran her smooth hand over his face. "Is he going to be okay?" she asked Pan.

"Of course he is," Pan said and to William asked, "Are there usually guards outside the prison?"

"You mean there aren'?"

"That's what I was afraid of. I think someone knows we're here. We have to get back to your family as quickly as possible."

"Jacob, can you hear me?" Alice bent close to his ear hoping to stir him from his slumber.

"Are the two of ya Orns?" William asked after getting a closer look at Pan and Alice.

"Yes and you're going to come live in the Goldwood Forest if we ever get out of here."

"Live with the Orns? Sounds mighty fine."

Jacob's eyes fluttered open, and Alice nearly screamed again, this time with delight. "You scared me to death, Jacob!"

"I'm all right, all right. Did it work?"

"It worked, but we have to get out of here, Jacob," Pan said. "Can you stand?"

"'Course I can stand." He attempted standing and would have fallen back to the ground if Alice hadn't caught him.

"Okay, let's go. I'm afraid we've been discovered, Jacob."

"You may be right, but I used all the magic I had getting him out," Jacob said.

"I guess we'll have to get out on pure skill then."

The four walked out of the building and found the streets just as deserted as before, but the noise from the pub had died as well, leaving only that sense of foreboding. They walked along the same path back to William's house. Once outside of his house, they sensed that something was wrong. They paused outside of the house and listened.

"Oh, how surprised they'll be to see me here," a familiar voice said. A high-pitched laugh followed.

"We shouldn't be here," Pan whispered to Jacob.

"But his family is in there," Jacob said back. "We can't leave them."

"He's right," said Alice, "I'm going with him."

"Whose voice is that?" Jacob asked Pan.

"I don't know. It's familiar, isn't it?"

"Do you think it's the traitor?"

"Must be. Be on guard"

Jacob rushed up the door of William's house. He knocked once more and heard Lorrie ask who it was.

"It's Jacob, Lorrie."

"Come on in, dear," she said back, her voice quivering only slightly as she spoke.

He opened the door and crossed the threshold. He had time to see Lorrie and her two sons sitting in chairs being guarded by what looked like a dark-haired Orn when two soldiers grabbed him from behind. He struggled and Pan came to his rescue. Four other soldiers jumped out of their hiding places to engage the two Orns. William stood helplessly in the doorway without a sword to fight.

Pan quickly killed one soldier with his sword while another tried to grab him. Jacob attempted to fight back against the two soldiers, but they managed to bind him with rope to a chair before returning to help their fellows. Alice stood frozen, sword in hand, watching the fight. Pan killed two more soldiers before they knocked his sword from his hand. One soldier lifted his sword to Pan's neck, and at last, Alice's paralysis broke.

She knocked the sword from the soldier's hand and doubled back to slice his throat. The final two soldiers came after Alice at the same time. One sank to the ground with Alice's sword stuck in his belly, while the other fell to the ground after a blow to the jaw from Pan's massive fist.

"That is enough," the dark-haired Orn said. He held a knife to Lorrie's throat and small rubies appeared on her skin where the knife pierced her flesh. "Any more movement and I will kill her."

Jacob, helplessly tied to the chair, stared at the Orn in disbelief. He recognized him although his features had changed, distorted. His hair was darker and his small vine tattoos began to creep up his neck.

Pan faced the Orn and rage lit up his face. "Luminous? You're the traitor?"

"Ah, Pan, finally you learn the secret. How it has taken you so long, I have no idea."

"But why would you choose King Ro over your own people?"

"The king has promised me great fortune and power. I went to see his Majesty shortly after he killed his wife, realizing the prophecy that Elda made would come true. I told him everything; he rewarded me greatly, teaching me much about Black Magic."

"So it was you I saw in the crowd at the ceremony?" Jacob asked.

"I was afraid when I learned that you could see the true essence of everything that you would find out who I was. I didn't realize that my identity would still be well preserved. Tell me, Jacob, what kept you from knowing it was me?"

Jacob fought the nightmare memory. But he let it fall through his mind. He knew he would have to confront the monster if he wanted to escape this.

"There is nothing left of your former self." He closed his eyes. "Not one ounce of good is left in you. You're only a black mass with red eyes. Horrible red eyes."

The smile on Luminous' face went slack. He stared at the boy, and for one moment, his vulnerability showed. Alice saw it and acted on a Warrior's instinct. She hurled her sword at him, while he continued to stare at Jacob. The sword curved to the left of its target, embedding itself in Luminous' right arm.

He howled in pain, releasing the knife from Lorrie's neck to attempt to pull the sword from his arm. William rushed to his wife, Alice rushed to Jacob, and Pan rushed after Luminous. After a few slashes of the knife, William's family was free, and Alice worked the ropes off of Jacob. Pan grabbed hold of the traitor before he could successfully pull the sword free.

"How could you?" he screamed. "All of those Orns that lost their lives. How could you turn your back on your own people?"

For the first time, Luminous showed true fear.

"Pan, I meant none of it, I swear. I only wanted a better life."

"Lies! Get out of my sight, you lying dog." Pan shoved him, and Luminous stumbled over his own feet. The sword fell from his arm, and blood poured out of the wound. "Go find your king, maybe he can fix your arm."

"I can't go to him. He'll kill me. I've already promised him Jacob, and he's on his way here at this moment."

Those words sent the alarm through Jacob. "We have to go. Now!"

They didn't stop to think about it. At Jacob's words, they all darted out of William's house, except Pan. He stayed back with Luminous.

"Show me mercy, Pan, kill me. Make it quick. The king won't."

Pan's voice bounced off the walls of the small house as he responded, "That's what you deserve. When he's boiling the flesh off your bones, you remember those six Orn women that you sold to King Ro for just a little bit of power."

"I didn't know what he had planned for them, honest, Pan."

"I told you not to lie to me!" Pan's leg flew out and connected with the side of Luminous' head. The force of the kick rolled Luminous onto his back, and that's where he lay until the king found him later.

"Let's go," Pan said as soon as he emerged from the house. He led the way through the streets of the town right up to the gate. Ham and his companions had not returned to their posts after their last confrontation with Jacob, Pan, and Alice.

Once the party cleared the gate, they ran. Jacob took a look toward the king's city and thought he saw small torches on the horizon heading toward them. "They're coming," he said. "Luminous wasn't lying."

"We should be on our way home by the time the king gets here, we just have to get to the horses," Pan assured him.

They reached the horses after a few minutes. Jacob hopped onto Alice's horse with her, while Pan rode with the two boys, and William and Lorrie shared Jacob's horse. They rode for the border of the forest, trying to outrun the death that loomed behind them.

As they rode, Jacob fought the urge to look back over his shoulder to see how much ground the king's party gained.

They rested for a few hours after they'd reached the edge of the forest. Then as they prepared to leave, some of the largest trees around them collapsed into great piles of gray sand. A great black cloud of smoke erupted on the horizon, right over the black castle, and they knew that King Ro had made it home.

"He's started," Pan said.

"Wha's he started?" William asked.

"The Uruk Taki," Jacob whispered, the black smoke reflected in his huge eyes.

Chapter 17

The Hall of Histories

They entered the Treetop City sometime around midday. Exhaustion washed over the party, but their safety made them happy. Jacob planned to sleep for a few hours then go with Pan to the council hall to inform the Tribesmen of all they learned on their journey. Pan believed that the Tribesmen would find their information useful and that the war with King Ro drew ever nearer to beginning.

During most of the ride in the forest William's family remained quiet. The loss of their home and the old lives gave them great pain. They expressed their gratitude at having a new place to live and for the freedom they could now live with, but their entire married lives had been spent in that house. It was the only home that Francis and Harold had ever known.

Pan showed William and his family a tree furnished with beds where they would live. He commanded them to get some sleep and for William to enjoy some time with his family after being away from them for so long.

"I want ta fight agains' the king, understand?" he told Pan when his family had safely gone inside.

"Yes. You will be allowed to join our fighting force," Pan said.

"I jus' can' believe that the boy I foun' on the side o' the road saved me. If it'd been me, I'da left me." He hung his head to show his remorse.

"Doesn't matter, William, you saved me, and I returned the favor," Jacob said.

William lifted his head slightly to Jacob to show that he'd heard and backed quickly into his new house. As soon as the door closed, Regal came out of the trees, swinging on a vine. He bowed low before Pan.

"My lord," he said, "I found Luthos' body just before nightfall last night. He'd been murdered. I mourned him until the Odds came to take him away. And his brother Luminous is missing."

Pan sighed. "I feared as much. Luthos was a good warrior. He will be missed. As for Luminous, I don't think we'll be seeing him for quite some time."

Regal looked into his captain's eyes for some sort of explanation, but it was clear that none would be given.

Pan turned to Jacob. "I will see you in a few hours."

Jacob walked with Alice down to her house. Again they separated for their own bedrooms, but after only a few minutes, Alice came to Jacob's room.

"Jacob, this can't be the way," Alice said after she entered his room.

"If this wasn't the way then why did you come to my world in the first place? You knew I was the only hope."

"I know. But I didn't think I would feel this way about you when the time finally came for the battle."

"We don't even know if we'll be fighting, and I don't know how to destroy the Uruk Taki yet. The war won't begin until I'm prepared, I hope."

"All of this is just so frightening. Can I just stay here and talk with you?"

"Of course."

And they talked. For nearly three hours, they sat on the bed in Jacob's room and talked about everything. Jacob told her stories about his brother and his dad that he missed so much. He even confessed to her about his imaginary brother. She didn't laugh but seemed to understand what Jacob meant.

Alice told him about growing up in Toratoga, the colors of the forest, and how she always looked up to her sister, Aural. Jacob listened intently, letting his apprehension of the coming battle melt away. He felt more at home having a conversation with Alice in a different world than he'd ever felt in Oklahoma.

When Pan came to get them a few hours later, Jacob didn't want to move. Staring into Alice's eyes, everything seemed right in the world.

"I hate to disturb the two of you, but Jacob, you need to come with me. The Tribesmen will be in council shortly, and you are the main guest," Pan said.

Jacob gave Pan a smile and reluctantly gave up his spot in the bed. Alice obviously didn't want the conversation to end either, but she let her hero go.

On the road of the Treetop City, very few Orns were out. The sun had just begun to set, and most of the citizens of Treetop City were already preparing for bed. Ludlum continued to stand guard at the door of the council hall, but said nothing as Pan and Jacob passed to enter.

Once more, the Tribesmen sat behind the table, the eerie grey firelight lit the room, and a few Warriors stood along the wall. Jacob and Pan stopped in the middle of the room.

"Why are we here tonight, Pan?" Galadawn asked. Despite the fact that he'd been cleared as the traitor, Jacob could still feel some kind of loathing for the old Orn.

"Jacob and I have witnessed the birth of a great cloud of smoke over the black castle. We believe the king has begun creating the Uruk Taki." He quickly told the Tribesmen of their journey to the south and how they narrowly avoided the king.

"You went to the Smoketown without our permission?" Galadawn asked, anger pouring into every word.

"I think that is the least of our worries right now, Galadawn," Elda said. "We've trusted Pan as our Captain all this time, and I believe we can trust his judgment when it comes to these matters." The other Tribesmen murmured their agreement.

"Very well, Elda, you've spoken against me enough, I think you can run these meetings without me." Galadawn stood and left the council hall through the back door. When the door closed, a steady silence rang through the hall.

"We had no intention of causing that," Pan said.

"He's been acting that way ever since Jacob came here. His hatred of outsiders makes him so difficult to work with," Elda said. "Now, Jacob, did you fix the ring?"

Jacob lifted his right hand to show the Orns the ring. "Yes."

"Then we are ready."

"But how do I destroy the Uruk Taki?"

"Using the ring, Jacob. I believe there are records in the Hall of Histories on how Lothlor defeated them."

"Where is it?"

"On the south side of the city. You may go there after the horn is blown."

"Is it likely that I will face the Uruk Taki?"

"Not if we beat King Ro to it. Captain Pan, gather your troops. Sound the horn to send word to Methindail to gather the Elves. We march on the Black Castle at the break of day. Are you ready, Pan?"

"More than ever."

"Good, now go forth. And, Jacob, do not fear what you do not know will happen. This war may be over in just a few minutes."

"But it won't."

"No, probably not, but even I cannot predict how it will turn out. Go."

Pan and Jacob left the hall and walked down the street of Treetop City. Pan led Jacob to the northern part of the city, a part Jacob had yet to see. They walked along for a while, when Pan stepped off the main road onto one of the many sidewalks. Soon they came to a large tree with no branches. The trunk had been carved and hallowed into two large horns. About five feet above the sidewalk, protruding out of the trunk, was the mouth piece for the horns.

"A blast from this horn will call the entire forest into battle, including the Elves," Pan said. "All will know it's time. Would you blow the horn, Jacob?"

"Me?" Jacob felt suddenly smaller than he ever had. "You want me to wake the entire forest?"

"That is why you're here, is it not? To lead us into battle?"

"Yeah, I guess it is."

Jacob walked up to the horn and blew with all of his might. The noise that rang forth shook the very sidewalk he stood on, and every leaf rattled, some falling free from their homes to land on the dirt of the ground. Jacob's cheeks deflated and the sound of the horns died, except for the distant echoes of it.

"We should hear a reply," Pan said. After a few moments, they heard the ringing of the answering horn blast. "Yes, the Elves will join us in battle, Jacob."

On the eve of the great battle, the fear, excitement, and trepidation hung over the city like some great shadow that blocked out all light and snuffed the hope of a new day. When the battle was weeks, maybe even months away, there was no question that the Orns would dominate, but the night before the war broke, doom lurked around them.

The city stirred at the sound of the great horn. Every Orn rose out of bed and went out into the streets, some looking frightened, others excited. Many were already at work, preparing arrows and spears, and yet, many others found the horn blast to be so frightening that it angered them. They stormed from neighbor to neighbor demanding to know who sounded the alarm and if it was necessary.

Of course, it *was* necessary. If they wanted their world back to the way it was before, they had to fight for it.

Jacob wandered the streets, alone. Pan left him to gather his troops on the underside of the city, so Jacob walked to the southern part of the city to visit the Hall of

Histories. He felt it was his final training before going into battle and he never felt more alone; he was glad to have the company of his brother in his mind, the constant companion through his toughest days.

No one bothered him; in fact, most didn't even notice the boy. He walked among the Orns as one of them, and yet, not quite a part of them. At last, he reached the southern part of the city, and for the most part, it was clear of all Orns. Only a few still hung about their houses, waiting and watching.

At the end of the road stood a brilliant tree. Ornate pictures carved into the wood in various places, decorated the outside of it. Jacob saw different scenes depicted in each of the pictures. One showed a Grebble bearing down on a group of small Orn children; another showed a great Orn standing with his bloody sword raised in triumph. The last one Jacob could see showed a small boy looking lost and afraid. He didn't even have to look at the boy's right hand to know that he only had nine fingers. It was a picture of him.

What is this place?

"I don't know, but I'm going in."

You sure you should?

"Now you're afraid?"

No, but what if it's dangerous?

"How can it be in the Treetop City? This has to be the Hall of Histories"

Jacob pushed the door in the great trunk open and entered the strange tree. He entered a dimly lit room with a few small candles around the walls. There were a few chairs, but mostly bookshelves lined the walls. Jacob could see shapes of people standing at the end of the room. He walked toward them, noticing just how loud each of his footsteps sounded in the room. The people, as it turned out, were simply statues, carved from the wood of the tree. He studied each one of them, but after a moment, realized he was no longer alone.

"Who's there?" He turned around quickly, drawing his sword at the same time.

"So you've found the Hall of Histories." Jacob knew that voice. He couldn't quite place it, but suddenly fear ignited in him.

"Where are you?"

"This room contains some of the oldest magic known to Toratoga. The original inhabitants of this city built it, and the magic continues to course through in the way that they designed. You noticed the picture of yourself outside, did you not?"

He could almost picture the owner of the voice, but suddenly he was curious about the room. "Yes, I noticed. How did it get there?"

"The Orns who built this room designed it to keep track of everything that goes on in the Goldwood Forest. Every historical aspect of the Treetop City and the woods around it. They didn't want to keep track of it on their own, but they were so obsessed with recording their own history. My guess is that they were afraid that it would repeat itself."

"What happened in the histories?"

"A human child wandered into our world and nearly destroyed it. The picture of the Orn with the bloody sword raised is Lothlor. He killed the corrupt human."

"I thought the last time anything like this happened, the king's servant brought it about."

"Yes, the king was obsessed with the other worlds so when a boy wandered into our world, he wanted to be around him at all times. Eventually the boy grew up and became very tired of the king. He killed him and the world lost its color."

Suddenly Jacob recognized the anger in the voice. He remembered the only time he'd ever heard that voice was in the Council Hall with the Tribesmen. "Galadawn?"

"You've come to it at last." The frail shape of the old Orn stepped out of the darkness, so that Jacob could see him. "I am the only one of the Tribesmen who comes to this room. I am the only one who knows the histories of this world. I am the only one who knows the truth about your father."

"My dad? You mean all that he did to help the Orns?"

"Yes, he did so much to help us. He also did what you see around us. He sent this world into a tailspin."

Jacob couldn't believe the old Orn. He stood in silence as the Galadawn spoke.

"He first came into our world several years ago. He continued to come back, and out of curiosity, I followed him. He'd met a girl, you see. A young woman about his own age. A human girl, not of the Goldwood Forest. He was quite taken with her, I believe.

"Their love blossomed. But your father would have to return home. He would constantly leave her and his visits became less and less frequent. His friendship with Pan had also blossomed over the years, so I watched them.

"Your father confessed to Pan that he'd met Mary-Anne in his world and that he'd gotten her pregnant. He told Pan that he would marry her and probably wouldn't be able to come back to our world anymore. Pan made sure your father got that ring, so that he could visit whenever he wanted."

He stared at the ring for a moment, considering it. Then he continued, "He only came back once, and that was to tell Pan that your brother was born. Meanwhile, the woman he'd been seeing here had also gotten married to the prince. Shortly after your father's last visit, the king died, and the prince became the king. Yes, my dear boy, your father was once in love with King Ro's wife. When he broke her heart by never returning for her, she married Ro. She was miserable and never seemed to get over your father. Ro, himself, was happy with her. Then the affair came."

Jacob listened, understanding that it all made sense, but still refused to believe it. His dad couldn't have been responsible for all of this. At least that's what he thought.

He decided to stall Galadawn with different questions while he sorted out this new information in his mind. "How would the ring have helped him get here?"

"Oh, Jacob, you should know by now just how powerful those rings are. The bathtub portal you came through is only one of a few in your world. Wearing the ring, however, turns any tub of water into a portal to our land. Alice, of course, doesn't know any of this. We teach our young very little about the magic in our world."

"But how did my dad first get here?"

"He simply found one of the portals. Tell me, Jacob, did your father take lots of baths?"

Jacob didn't even have to think about it. His dad always took baths, very rarely using the shower unless he was in hurry. Jacob never thought it a strange behavior. "Yeah, all the time."

"I thought so. He missed Toratoga, you see, but he would never visit here again. He had a family to look after, and the temptation to see his old girlfriend might be too high. Plus, he'd given the ring away."

"He didn't give me the ring until a few months ago."

"You were not the first person he gave the ring to. He'd given it first to his brother, your uncle."

"Uncle Gail? No, he died out at sea or something. I never really knew him."

"Foolish boy. Your uncle lived in Toratoga. He lived here for two years when he caught the queen's eye. Great resemblance to your father, you see. Their affair lasted for quite some time before the king noticed it. They became reckless, feeling quite invincible in their lie. But as you know, he did finally catch them. He murdered them both."

"If my uncle had the ring then how did my father get it back?"

"That is my only problem. I was surprised to see you pull it from you pocket. I can't figure how it got from here to your world."

"You see? It couldn't have been my uncle."

"Oh, but it was. Gail Kepler. It's here in the histories. But right now, that is the least of your worries. I am going to undo all of this evil and prevent you from bringing anymore in."

Jacob barely had time to process what he'd just heard when Galadawn lunged at him, knife in hand. Finally, it became clear that Galadawn saw Jacob as the source of all the evil and meant to destroy him. Galadawn's mind had become warped from the evil in the land.

Jacob leapt to the side, just barely missed by Galadawn's outstretched hands. He couldn't believe how quickly the old Orn moved. The skinny fingers of the Orn were around Jacob's throat before he had time to turn around and in the excitement, Jacob's blade slipped from his hand. He saw the glint of the knife in the firelight as Galadawn raised it over his head. Jacob tried to move, but the Orn's hand had a firm grip on his neck.

The knife came down, aimed for Jacob's throat, but he managed to get his hand under it to fight the Orn. Galadawn pushed down on Jacob's arm, so that the knife pierced the skin of his shoulder. Jacob gasped as much as he could under the pressure in his throat when the knife cut his skin.

Suddenly, the Orn's eyes grew huge, and his hands fell slack at the sight of something on Jacob's shoulder. He began to back away. Jacob reached up and wrenched the knife out of his flesh, not sure why the Orn backed away from him. Dark red blood covered the end of the knife. Jacob looked at it with curiosity. Apparently more than just his eyes had regained their color during the fixing of the ring.

"What have I done?" Galadawn looked at the red blood on his hand. "He has color. His blood is red. It's just like it used to be. So beautiful." To Jacob's shock, Galadawn began to lick the blood from his hand, giggling softly to himself.

"Now I have the color. Yes, it's in me now." He appeared to have forgotten that Jacob was even in the room. Jacob watched the old Orn cautiously, holding the knife steadily in his hand, a scarlet drop of blood falling from the end of it. "Oh, I missed the color. It tastes so good.

"But the boy." The Orn looked up from his treat, blood smeared around his mouth, and his eyes caught Jacob's. "He'll tell. Yes, he will tell everyone. No one must know that I tried to kill him. No, they mustn't.

"Will they know that it was I that poisoned Luminous' mind? Will they come for me if they know that I set up the betrayal and the downfall of the Orns? Yes, I think they will."

"What are you saying madman?" Jacob felt a cold chill grip his heart. He heard everything the Orn said, but he sounded so out of his mind, so crazy, he didn't know whether he should believe it. But Galadawn continued to ignore Jacob.

He turned to walk out of the room and Jacob felt the relief wash over him. But faster than the flutter of a hummingbird's wing, Galadawn was after him. He turned back and leapt high into the air, aiming his jump to land on Jacob. His aim was good.

He landed on the boy, and the two fell to the ground. Galadawn let out a great scream, and Jacob rolled the Orn off of himself. In his madness, Galadawn had forgotten about the knife that now protruded from his chest. He raised his head so he could see the blood pooling in the wound around the blade. It was black.

He let out one final scream that echoed around the small room and died. Jacob stood over the body for a moment before walking out of the room. He saw a new picture on the wall once he got outside. It depicted a young warrior holding a knife in a battle against a great monster. Jacob thought he could see the resemblance of Galadawn in the monster's face.

As he began to walk away, the blue lights of the Odds descended into the Hall of the Histories.

Chapter 18

A Visitor in the Night

Pan came running out of the darkness followed by Regal and a few other Warriors. He saw Jacob walking and stopped short. The mess of red blood that smeared the boy's shoulder shocked him.

"Jacob, what's happened? We came as soon as we saw the Odds fall out of the sky."

Jacob barely noticed that Pan had said anything. He couldn't quite grasp what had just happened to him. Blue light fell over them as the Odds flew back into the sky, carrying their corpse between them.

"Jacob, what happened?" Pan grabbed Jacob's shoulders and shook. Jacob's eyes shifted to Pan and finally focused on him.

"Galadawn," Jacob mumbled. "He tried to kill me."

"What? Galadawn tried to kill you? What are you talking about?" Pan nodded at two of the Warriors with him to go on and search where Jacob had just come.

"He told me everything, Pan." Jacob's voice regained its strength as he spoke. "It was all my dad's fault. All of this. That's why I have to fix it, right? Fixing the mistakes my dad left behind."

"That's not true, Jacob. Your father didn't cause this."

"Then explain to me how my uncle got here to have the affair. My father's ring, right?" He held up his right hand. "This ring."

"You have to understand that he never intended for his brother to do anything like that. He was only trying to forget the memory of Toratoga while trying to raise his family. He was trying to be a good father, Jacob."

"Well, he sure succeeded, didn't he? Look how well I turned out."

"Calm down. You dad had no idea what would result from giving your uncle the ring. Think about it, Jacob, if you wanted to get rid of the ring, who would be the first person you would give it to?"

That thought struck Jacob hard. He suddenly realized his father's predicament. He'd simply given the coolest thing he'd ever owned to the coolest person he'd ever known. Jacob would have done the same thing in a moment. That explained the change that had come over his father at Gail's funeral. Things weren't the same at home after that.

Once again, a sheer determination to save Toratoga seared through his body. "You're right, Pan. I just wish I knew how he got the ring back after Uncle Gail died."

"Did you find out how Lothlor defeated the Uruk Taki?"

"I forgot all about it." Jacob turned away from Pan to head back to the Hall of Histories.

The two Warriors returned from inspecting the scene, so Jacob waited to hear what they said. "Captain, it appears they fought in the Hall of Histories. There is a new picture on the wall there depicting it."

Pan listened as the Warriors explained everything they'd seen. Jacob nodded his concurrence with each bit of information. Then something struck him as wrong.

"If everything in the Goldwood Forest is recorded in there, why didn't you ever look for the traitor among it?"

"We did, Jacob, but someone kept stealing the bits of parchment we needed. We would ask Galadawn who always seemed to be in there, but he never saw anyone.

"Do you think Galadawn took the evidence?"

"I wonder now, after what you've told me," Pan said.

Every eye of the Warriors bore into Jacob. They were having trouble believing that their head Tribesman had turned to evil. Jacob told them everything he heard while in the Hall of Histories with Galadawn, including when Galadawn spoke only to himself.

"He admitted to turning Luminous against us?" Pan's eyes were huge.

"I don't think he realized I was there. He was only speaking to himself, and he kept licking my blood."

"You've proven yourself a hero again, Jacob Nine-fingers. Now return to the Hall of the Histories. I will wait here for you."

Jacob ran back to the hall. A small chill rolled down his back when his eyes found the picture depicting him and Pan. With a slight tremble in his hand, he reached out to open the door again.

He walked among the books, checking each one, pulling them from their places and leafing through them. After giving a few books a quick look, he found one that said only "Lothlor" on the cover.

He pulled the book from its place and opened the old pages. The book told of the birth of Lothlor and how he quickly rose to title of Captain among the Orn Warriors. He was powerful and able to wield magic to do amazing things that other Orns found difficult.

At last Jacob found the pages he was looking for in the massive book. He read:

"When Hait, the human from the other world, killed King Anan, Toratoga began to destroy itself. All lost the power to wield magic; all except Lothlor. Somehow he could still use magic and every living thing in Toratoga rallied around him to defeat the evil Hait.

"But Hait managed to create the Uruk Taki using Black Magic. The six beasts came out of the castle and began killing multitudes of the forces against Hait. The hope of conquest rested fully on the shoulders of Lothlor.

"He acquired as much magic as he could possibly carry, storing as much as he could in his ring as well. When he faced the six Uruk Taki on the field of battle, he maneuvered around the defenses of each one. He sent all of the magic through his ring. His right index finger turned the green of the stone, and he simply touched the Uruk Taki with the magical finger. The high concentration of pure magic in that finger destroyed the Black Magic that created the Uruk Taki.

"Without the Uruk Taki, Hait was defenseless. Lothlor took his life and returned Toratoga to its original form. Lothlor became the first and only Orn king of Toratoga."

192

Jacob closed the book and replaced it on the shelf. He tried to still his shaking limbs. He touched the stub that was left instead of a finger. All he needed was magic, a ring, and his index finger to touch the monsters. He couldn't help but feel disheartened at the fact that he didn't have a right index finger. He finally left the hall and rejoined Pan and the other Warriors.

Jacob walked amid the Warriors back to the center of the town. Alice found them and nearly lost it when she saw all the blood on Jacob's shoulder. Jacob had forgotten all about it. Her mother sewed it up and bandaged it for him. Alice insisted that they take a walk around the forest floor for a little while.

They reached the ground of the forest and began to walk to the north. A few Orn Warriors stood guard on the ground along with some of the human soldiers, and a few elves were beginning to show up, also.

Jacob saw William standing next to one tree talking with an Orn Warrior. They waved, but Alice kept him on their walking path. She grabbed his hand and he held onto it gratefully. There was something so calming about the touch of Alice's hand. Jacob's breathing slowed, and for the first time since blowing the horn, he felt the fear dwindle.

"Jacob, you coming here, you've changed my life," Alice said in a quiet voice when they were well away from anyone that might hear.

"You've definitely changed my life, Alice."

"I feel so different around you. Like, I don't know, like I could breathe under water if you asked me to. That sounds silly."

"But describes it perfectly."

Alice stopped walking. Jacob stopped. They stood in the heart of the forest, staring into one another's eyes.

"Do you mean it, Jacob?" Alice took a step closer to him.

To answer her, he grabbed her in his arms and kissed her. Their kiss only lasted a moment when they were disturbed by someone speaking to Jacob without making a sound. He heard in his head only his name, and he broke his embrace with Alice. When he turned around, Elea stood behind him.

The Anjel relaxed his wings against his back, but to Jacob, his pure white body looked out of place in the forest. "I have caught you at a bad time, I apologize." The voice rang through Jacob's head just as it had at the ceremony.

"No need for that. Why have you come here?"

"To give you warning. No, Alice, you may hear this also." Jacob turned back and saw that Alice had begun to walk away. He reached out to her and grabbed her hand. She looked gratefully at him.

"What are you warning me?"

"The Uruk Taki."

"I know, the king is working on making them."

"He has already created three, Jacob."

"*Three*? Already?"

"Only you have the power to defeat them, Jacob. Swords and arrows cannot harm them. I suggest that you focus your strength and energy on them. You've read how to defeat them, correct?"

Jacob stole a glimpse at his missing finger. "Yeah, I read it."

"Then you are prepared. Just get to them before they get to you. Be quick and dodge every blow they deliver.

194

And, Jacob, do not worry about what you lack. Just do what you know is right."

"Will the Anjels fight with us?"

"No, Jacob, as I told you before, this fight does not concern us."

"But you're here now."

"I found something in you that I have not seen in many. You have the desire to go forth into this battle even though you know what it will cost you. You show a great strength and courage."

"Can you not convince the other Anjels to join in with you?"

"I do not believe anything will make them come out of their homes. They have very little to do with this world, and prefer it to remain that way. You have more than enough on your side to defeat King Ro. Just defeat the Uruk Taki first."

"Thank you, Elea. Will you be watching out for us tomorrow?"

"Of course. Look for me in the sky when you need it most. Until tomorrow, Jacob Nine-fingers."

The great black wings spread out from the Anjel's back and with a flick of those wings, he rose into the air, flying up through the tops of the trees and out of sight. Jacob bent his head all the way back to watch the Anjel go, still clutching Alice's hand.

Alice, however, looked at Jacob. "What did he mean, Jacob? 'You know what it will cost you.'"

Jacob jumped out of his trance. "I don't really know."

"Jacob." She grabbed his face and made him look into her eyes. "What did he mean?"

He could not turn his gaze away from those purple eyes. "He told me that the war will take everything from me."

"Do you mean...you will die?" Tears formed in her eyes.

"I don't know what he meant. He only told me that some things must happen for the greater good."

"Jacob, you tell me right now what that means."

"I can't Alice, that's all he told me." They were standing close enough for him to feel her heart beat, and he was afraid his own would give something away to her. He felt that the war would kill him. He would defeat the evil, but he would die. Of course, he couldn't tell Alice that.

She dropped her eyes from him, and pushed her face against his chest. He felt the truth beginning to form on his tongue. He felt bad for lying to her and wanted to tell her. But before he could, another horn blast shook the ground. The sun would be up soon, and the time to march to the black castle had come.

Chapter 19

March on the Black Castle

The Warriors gathered at the bottom of the Treetop City, many seeing it for the last time. Among the Warriors stood several of the king's soldiers who'd left his army to fight against him. Their presence among the Orns sparked a hope in the crowd, proof of rebellion against the king.

Methindail led his Elves out onto the ground of the forest with the Orns. They pulled their dark cloaks up around their shoulders, concealing their weapons of swords, bows and arrows. The Elves would rain the arrows down on the king's soldiers, as they were the best marksmen in Toratoga.

Pan stood at the front of the great crowd of Warriors. When Jacob joined the throng, Pan beckoned him to stand at the front. Once Jacob joined Pan, his knees nearly gave out from the sight of the massive army in front of him. He missed just how big the Orn population was, and the Elves more than doubled the size of the army. Pan held up his hands for silence.

"Warriors, Elves, and soldiers," he said, his voice ringing out over the crowd. "Today we march for the Black Castle. This is not another battle. This is not another skirmish against the king. This is war!" The army erupted in a great roar that almost knocked Jacob off his feet.

"Today we march against King Ro one final time. He will make his last stand, but he will fall. We will fight with more passion, with more vigilance, and we will fight to gain our world back from a corrupt overlord." Once more the army erupted in a roar.

"We have a hope, a guiding light that King Ro does not have. We have pure magic, and it's in the form of the Nine-fingered boy." This time the army erupted in such a roar that the trees behind Jacob seemed to bend from the force of it. Pan could certainly get the crowd excited.

"Listen." Pan looked surprised at the sound of Jacob's voice, so clear over the roar of the crowd. Jacob looked more surprised than Pan. "We march into dangers most have not seen in Toratoga. We march into the very outstretched arms of Death. But still we march!"

Pan led the eruption of voices from the crowd. When they finally quieted, Jacob only had one last thing to say.

"The time has come, Elves, Orns, and Humans. Fight not for me or for yourselves, but for your homes, that you may come back to them and see them bleeding with color."

Excitement thundered through the army, and they set off, toward the Great War against King Ro. Regal led the horse riders through the path in the woods that Pan, Jacob, and Alice had taken. Jacob marched with the Warriors, among the Warriors, as a Warrior. Pan led them through the Goldwood Forest, around Lake Kelpie, to the very edges of the woods. As one, the great sea of fighters stepped out onto the grey desert sand that was once a part of their forest.

By the time every Warrior stood on the desert sand, the sun had already begun its descent in the sky. They camped on the edge of the forest for the night, finding their last bit of comfort near the trees.

They set up tents, tied up the horses, and built small fires scattered throughout the campground. Soon the night air was full of the sounds of Orns, Elves, and Humans, laughing, eating, and drinking. The thoughts of war were well away from them and their fears slumbered for the evening.

Jacob walked among the army, watching a few, listening to others. Some beckoned him to join them, while others simply stared at the wondrous boy. Somehow in the mess, he found Pan, laying back next to a warm fire, and snoozing lightly. Jacob woke him.

"What is it, Jacob?" Pan asked, his voice groggy, and sounding more than a little annoyed at having been woken up.

"I am sorry, Pan, but I have one small question."

"Go ahead."

"I read that Lothlor stored magic in his ring that aided him in the defeat of the Uruk Taki. How do I do that?"

Pan sat up, eyes ablaze with what Jacob had told him. "He stored magic in his ring?"

"That's what I read."

"I've never thought of it. I've never tried, and I've never known anyone who has."

"So you mean it's not possible?"

"No, I'm sure it's possible. If you read it in the histories, it has to be true."

"What should I do then?"

"I don't know, Jacob. You'll have to figure it out."

Disheartened once again, Jacob set off for the trees to gather as much magic as he possibly could. He walked among the shadows, touching different tree trunks to gather some magic from each one. He would feel the familiar tingle travel up his arm and disperse into his body, and he would move on to the next one.

After touching ten trees, he could no longer feel a tingle. He'd filled up with as much as he could. Then there was the problem of loading magic into the ring. He thought about it only a moment before he did the logical thing: he touched the stone of the ring to a tree.

As soon as the stone came into contact with the tree, it lit up like a bright green beacon in the dark shadows. The ring began to shake as the magic passed around and around the circle of metal. The amount of magic coursing through Jacob became so intense that his eyes began to glow just like the stone. Once again, he thought he saw the faintest traces of green at the end of his stub, but it must have just been the light.

The shaking of the ring subsided as it took its fill of magic. He pulled his hand away from the tree, and looked at the still glowing stone. He was able to feel the slight tingle of the magic flying around in the ring. He was ready for the battle.

He continued to walk among the woods for a little while longer, relishing the safety and comfort the trees brought. Fear taunted him. If the battle began the next day, he was sure that would be his last day. No matter how brave he felt at the idea of marching into battle, he still felt the fear of the unknown that came along with death.

He finally went back to the camp after a few hours. The army slept, and the fires dwindled to nothing. Pan decided that a lookout wasn't needed this far from the enemy, so all found rest that night. All except Jacob.

Once he stood among the army once more, he looked about for a place to sleep for the rest of the night. Clouds parted in the sky, and the moonlight spilled forth from its hiding place, giving Jacob enough light to see around him. His heart took a sudden lurch as his eyes caught a hint of blue just a few yards from the campground.

The Grebble wandered the desert and happened upon the army. He chanced a closer look to estimate the number of their forces. That's when the moonlight caught his skin and Jacob saw.

"Grebble!" he screamed, trying to rouse as much of the army as he could in case more Grebbles hung about in the shadows.

Several Orns jumped up, swords in hand, ready for the battle, but Jacob's scream had alerted the Grebble that someone had seen him. The Orns searched about the desert, but the blue beast was already gone. They found footprints in the sand, proof that only one Grebble had found them. A thick silence came over the camp. King Ro would now be warned of their coming, and he would be ready. They no longer held the element of surprise.

Pan set out twenty guards to watch for any more activity on the edges of the campground. He felt a deep resentment at his own actions for not placing the guard sooner. To stifle some of the guilt, he joined the guard to watch over the army.

The night went on without further intrusion but a lingering sense of alarm loomed among the fighters.

They set off the next morning at sunrise and marched further across the desert. Jacob sought Pan out of the crowd and spoke to him.

"Pan, does it hurt to die?"

"Why would you ask that, Jacob?"

"I have a bad feeling about today. Does it hurt?"

"I wouldn't know, but I think there is the possibility that it would be painful to be stabbed. But the pain wouldn't last long. It would be gone as soon as you died."

"So the cause of death might be painful, but dying itself wouldn't be?"

"That would be my guess. And it looks like we will all find out, very soon."

Jacob followed Pan's gaze and found the great black army emerging over the horizon to enter the grey desert. Their number was great, and looked like a tremendous black cloud moving over the ground. After being in Toratoga, preparing and waiting for the war to begin, King Ro finally brought it to him. And all he could think about was his mother, his father, and his brother. He missed home more than ever, but home seemed so far away as he watched the evil king ride ahead of his army on the great black steed.

The Great War of Toratoga began.

Chapter 20

The Great War

Jacob's head cleared, his senses heightened, and his fears diminished. He'd thought about the war against King Ro everyday since meeting Alice for the first time at the end of Ash Street. He dreamed up different conclusions to the confrontation, each one resulting in his conquering of the great evil of Toratoga. The day had finally come for Jacob's dreams, his thoughts, to leap from his mind and land in reality.

The two armies marched toward each other, crossing the great expanse of desert. All of King Ro's army wore black armor, including the Grebbles. And as they neared the forest dwellers' army, Jacob could see the dreaded Uruk Taki.

The king rode his stallion in front of the army, his white robes and hair flashing in the sunlight. The monsters he'd created out of the destroyed bodies of Orn women marched beside him, equaling the height of him on top of his steed. They were greater than Jacob could believe.

As their features became clearer, he could see that the combination of the Orn women and Black Magic made a mockery of the beautiful Grebbles that they once were. The distortion wreaked havoc on their faces, mutating their features. Their muscles rippled under black and blue skin. They wore no armor and only carried a great mace with a spiked ball on the top. Jacob could feel his fear beginning to return.

The armies finally stopped their march when only eight-hundred yards separated them. The number of King Ro's army greatly outnumbered the forest dwellers. And they were fiercer. The battlefield stood between the armies, waiting patiently to drink their blood. The sun inched down the sky as afternoon began. The cold wind swept over the grey sand, and the armies waited. The sweet scent of the Grebbles drifted lazily over the field, tempting the noses of every Orn, elf, and soldier.

At last, King Ro rode forward on his mount, and broke the silence. "You've chosen death, you fools." His neck strained with each word he spoke. "We do not have to shed any more blood because of your stupidity. Just lay your weapons down and all will be forgiven."

"Why should we back down?" Pan's voice rang out over the battlefield. "We have our army with the better fighters, and we have more of a reason to fight."

"Very well, you have chosen, but know your fate." He held his right hand out, and a horseman broke out of the group and stopped next to the king. He pulled up a black bag and held it out to King Ro. The king reached his hand into the bag and jerked a round object from inside. Jacob's stomach did a few flips when he realized it was the head of Luminous, the traitor.

"You will join him today." The king hurled the severed head toward the forest dwellers. "Let it begin!" King Ro returned to the safety of his Uruk Taki and waited for the first move. The soldier who'd ridden out to hand King Ro the head continued to sit in the middle of the battlefield, waiting.

Pan gazed down at the severed head of his former comrade and gave the slightest of nods. The moment the gesture was made, an arrow flew from the army into the soldier's eye. His body went rigid, and he slipped from his horse. The sand got its first taste of blood that afternoon as the soldier died in its arms.

The battle began.

With a hard blow on his horn, Pan's Warriors rushed out in the open field, and Methindail's elves let the sky fill with their arrows that came raining down on the king's men. King Ro wasted no time in charging to meet Pan's army.

The clash shook the ground as the armies finally met in the middle of the field. The king's army fought with gleaming blades that rang out through the air as they struck against the forest dwellers' swords. Many of the elves' arrows found their mark, and those soldiers fell to the ground with the wooden shafts protruding from their bodies.

Jacob rushed into the battle with his sword drawn, ready to take out his anger and frustration on any who neared him. He fought with a passion, slaying three soldiers before getting remotely winded. As his passion grew, the stone in the ring brightened, and the magic in his body stirred.

Regal brought the horsemen forward, and the king's own horsemen met them in a horrendous battle. The king himself rode forward and met Regal in the fight. King Ro held a great black blade that twisted more than the tattoos that now covered his face. It was an evil looking blade, and Regal felt the full force of it as King Ro brought it down again and again.

"I will kill you all," King Ro shouted at Regal, each word falling between each sword strike he delivered. The king's speed surprised Regal, and at last got the better of him.

He knocked the king's sword away and, thinking he had the upper hand, brought his sword up even with King Ro's head. But before his blade landed on its mark, the black blade dove into the flesh of his chest. His arm fell to his side, his hand losing its grip on the sword, and his eyes stared at the gaping wound in his chest, the blood spilling out over his clothes and his horse. He couldn't quite believe the king had gained the upper hand so quickly. The king moved to fight another before Regal had even fallen from his horse.

Jacob saw Regal fall, and his heart cried out. He wanted to chase after King Ro right then, but three Orn Warriors flew past, blood spraying the air as they went. The three Uruk Taki entered the battle and Jacob's moment of heroism had come at last.

He dashed through the small battles going on around him and reached the first of the great beasts. The top of his head barely reached the thigh of the monster, and the stench that came off it reminded him of burnt food. As soon as he neared it, the great mace it carried flew at him. He dodged it easily, just sliding out of its way. He ran forward and dove for the monster.

He saw the mace coming at him as he flew through the air. The great spiked ball came within inches of him when it froze. He seized the moment so that everyone on the battlefield froze along with the mace. He continued his forward motion, his right hand extended to touch the Uruk Taki. He concentrated on the magic flowing through his stub of a finger, and the green light he thought he'd seen so many times reappeared, only this time forming his missing index finger.

In that moment, he saw the true form of the Uruk Taki. It looked like a giant Grebble with twisted limbs and skin. On his face was a look of anguish. He was miserable. Jacob also thought he caught sight of a flash of white light.

He released the moment just as his magic finger made contact with the black flesh of the Uruk Taki. The magic spilled out of the finger and into the monster. The Uruk Taki disappeared immediately, but a sonic boom issued forth from where it stood, causing the ground to ripple in great waves. The whole fight took only a few seconds.

The moment Jacob hit the ground on the opposite side of where the Uruk Taki once stood, the final two monsters came after him. He felt their massive steps jolt the ground as they neared him. Around him, the battle continued to roar. Orn Warriors fell before Grebbles, and soldiers fell before elves. King Ro rode among them, his sword flying fast and sure, slaying many.

The Uruk Taki attacked him, and he moved with great speed, dodging each blow the monsters delivered with their great weapons. Blow after blow came Jacob's way, and each one he dodged, but the beasts became frustrated. They began throwing their fists out after him as well. Jacob dodged a few, but one connected with him full on. He hit the ground, the air blew out of his lungs, and his head spun.

One Uruk Taki saw the advantage and raised his mace into the air. As he brought it down, a glowing white blade caught the wooden handle and severed the spiked ball from the weapon. The ball flew out and landed on the back of a Grebble's head. The Uruk Taki had no time to move before that same blade shot through the air towards his chest.

Jacob lay on the ground amazed as the white blade pierced the skin of the great monster. A tremendous scream erupted through the field as the beast blasted to pieces around the blade. The body parts flew over the battling armies. Jacob looked at the blade's owner and his jaw gaped as he saw Elea, the Anjel, holding the hilt of the sword.

"Jacob, the other," the Anjel's voice said in his head. "Hurry."

The final Uruk Taki stood still only for a moment before swinging his mace at the Anjel. Jacob once more dove over the ground, right hand extended, and the green finger rising up out of the stub. The magic made contact with the black flesh, and once more, the beast disappeared with a resounding sonic boom. The Anjel dodged the blow of the mace, and the king howled in fury as he realized that Jacob had destroyed his precious Uruk Taki.

"You came," Jacob said to Elea in the quiet moment that followed the destruction of the Uruk Taki.

"Only for a moment." The Anjel spread his wings and flew back to the sky.

Jacob resumed the fight and couldn't believe the amount of Orns lying on the ground in bloody heaps. A furious passion lit up his insides as he swung his sword into Grebbles and soldiers, killing any who came near him. The king worked his way to face the boy once more.

A Grebble rushed forward to fight Jacob, but as the fight began, the black sword pierced the Grebble's chest. The beast fell to the ground, and in its place, stood the terrible King Ro. Blood splattered his once white robes, and his blade gleamed with the blood of his fallen enemies. Jacob's fears were gone. He faced his greatest foe at last. Killing the king would be the end of all of this madness.

"You've changed since I last saw you," the king said.

"As have you." Jacob could barely see the shadow of the king he'd met after arriving in Toratoga. The black tattoo completely covered any visible flesh

"Let's end this." The black blade swung through the air as soon as the words were out of King Ro's mouth. Jacob's blade caught the black blade, and the fight began.

They started slow, swinging their swords toward each other, but each blow caught by the other's defense. They got a feel for how each fought with the sword. Jacob learned that the king would be a formidable opponent in this fight.

Jacob began to swing harder and harder, trying to catch the king off guard. He threw his sword to the right and brought it back to King Ro's body, but the king caught it with his own blade. He built his momentum, setting the king back on the defense. Each step he took toward the king, the king took a step back. Their blades began to fly faster than the eye could see. Neither let down any defenses.

Pan saw the fight begin between the two and ran forward to see if he could help. He couldn't believe his eyes when he saw the speed of Jacob's offensive. He'd never seen anyone fight with that kind of intensity. For a brief moment, he let himself hope that all would be finished. The other battles on the battlefield began to break down as the armies stopped to watch the fight between their two leaders.

Jacob held his sword with both hands, using every skill he ever tried against his brother or Pan. He swung to the king's weak side and still couldn't break the defenses. His arms grew so tired that the king gave up on the defensive and started on the offense. Pan watched Jacob begin to back away from the king and his hopes began to fall.

Instead of growing tired like Jacob, the king's sword began to fly with a more fevered intensity. At last, he delivered a crushing blow to Jacob's sword, which forced the blade down to the boy's left, and knocked his right hand from holding the sword. Jacob raised his sword with his left hand to block another blow from the king, and the silver ring with the green stone slipped from the stub of his right index finger.

As soon as he felt it slip, his eyes broke away from King Ro to watch it fall to the ground. He heard Pan yell for him to watch out, but he never saw the blade from the king fall below his own extended blade and pierce him. He felt the pressure build in his chest, and a moment later, a horrible stinging sensation erupted through his body.

Finally, he tore his eyes away from the ring once it hit the grey desert sand and looked down at the wound in his chest. Red blood poured from the wound, and his face flushed. His legs suddenly became too weak to hold his body, and he fell, first to his knees, then onto his side.

Pan rushed forward and grabbed Jacob up in his arms. Everything went numb and quiet as he looked down into the boy's eyes. Jacob gave him a small smile.

"I'm sorry, Pan," he whispered, "I didn't win."

"Quiet now, Jacob."

"You were wrong, Pan. This doesn't hurt at all. I can't feel a thing."

Pan saw the ring sitting in the sand beside Jacob's arm. He grabbed and put it back on the stub of Jacob's finger. "There you go, Jacob. Now don't leave us."

Jacob lifted his head to look at the ring. The small smile grew slightly. "I'm sorry, Pan." His eyes closed and didn't open again.

Jacob Nine-fingers, hero of the Goldwood Forest, savior of Toratoga, died.

Chapter 21

The End of War

Several things happened at the moment Jacob died. The first was that the Goldwood Forest disappeared, collapsing into piles of sand as many trees had already done. The only trees left standing were those of the Treetop City and those where the elves made their homes. Evil, it seemed, had taken over.

Another was that Alice, who'd managed to sneak away from the city and near the battlefield, watched from a distance as Jacob fell. She just reached Pan when Jacob breathed his last. Anguish like she'd never known tore through her body. Rivers of tears flowed down her cheeks, and her breaths came with great strain.

The final thing was the blue lights began to descend from the sky. The Odds landed and began gathering their dead. Pan screamed in agony for them to leave the boy, but they wouldn't. Their skinless faces almost smiled when gazing upon Jacob's face. They wanted him for their own, and they would have him.

From behind, the Odds were beautiful women with jet black hair that hung between their shoulders. Their blue gowns flowed around them like water drifting down a creek. The bottoms of their gowns covered their feet that floated inches above the ground. When they turned, and revealed their faceless skulls, all thoughts of beauty fell away as fright took hold of the observer.

At last, Pan subsided and gave them Jacob's body. He held Alice as the Odds ascended to the sky with the Orns only hope of life.

When King Ro pulled his blade from the boy's body, it melted, leaving only the hilt in the king's hand. He dropped it, and while Pan and Jacob shared their last words, he slipped back into the crowd. He found his general and issued him one command, "Take them."

After the Odds took Jacob, Pan realized the battle was over. All of his Warriors laid down their swords and spears and submitted themselves to the king's army. Hope vanished with Jacob's life.

Pan watched as King Ro's army made each member of his own army sit on the ground with their hands over their heads. They began to make a move toward him, but he had no intention of letting them take him.

He looked at Alice and she nodded. Pan sheathed his sword and grabbed Alice's hand. He took off as soon as a soldier neared him to force him into imprisonment. They ran through the desert to the north, toward the Neverise Mountains. Five more Orn Warriors joined them; everyone else didn't see the point of running. King Ro would catch them.

The soldiers watched them run but didn't pursue. Without the towering trees in the way, the mountains were clearly visible on the horizon. They knew where the

Orn rebels would end up. They could send out a scouting party the next day to collect them.

Pan and Alice ran, barely noticing the other Orns who ran with them. They could see the Treetop City in the distance and Pan hoped to reach it. Without an army, he couldn't hope to hold any kind of defense against the king there. They would have to head to the mountains where the numerous caves would protect them.

As the sun descended, the lights in the city lit up the trees. Still the Orns ran. As the night wore on, it was clear that the Orn women worried about the war. The lights continued to burn on into the night. Pan and Alice reached it just as the sun began to peak out once more. They climbed up the stairs to stand on the streets.

Although exhausted, Pan knew what needed to be done. He lifted his horn, the captain's horn, to his lips and blew it. At once, the streets filled with the Orns left in the city. They rushed out to see their captain, for they knew his horn blast. They looked at him expectantly, but Pan could see the anguish in their faces. They knew that trouble had befallen the army.

"My fellow Orns," Pan shouted to ensure that all heard his voice. "Our hope has fallen. Jacob Kepler, the nine-fingered boy, died." Cries of outrage filled the air, but most were subdued. Shock permeated the crowd.

"The king is taking our people as prisoners. Our only choice is to run to the north. To take shelter in the Neverise Mountains. We still have kin there. I believe we have a better chance of protecting ourselves there."

This time, there were far more cries of outrage. The Treetop City was home to the Orns, and many couldn't grasp the idea of leaving it. Pan saw it in their eyes and heard it in their cries.

"If you choose not to leave with me, King Ro will force you to leave. He will imprison you and make you his slaves. If you choose to stay here, you choose death. Come with me. We can make a living for ourselves in the north."

As the crowd roared, one small voice spoke up. "Is there no other way, Captain?" Pan saw Elda come up through the crowd to address him.

"No, Elda, I'm afraid there isn't," he told her. She simply nodded and turned back into the crowd.

"I leave immediately. It won't be long before the Grebbles are upon you, and the king has control of you. If you want to come with me, come now."

Pan turned from the crowd and walked down the stairs, possibly for the last time in his life. Alice walked with him, as well as the five Orn Warriors who fled the battlefield with their captain. Among those Warriors was Ludlum, the Orn who stood guard over the council hall day after day. They left the city in silence.

By the end of the next day, Pan led the Orns across the expanse from the Treetop City to the caves in the Neverise Mountains. Two-hundred other Orns joined them from the city, including the eight remaining Tribesmen. All others remained behind because no more hope resided in them.

The northern Orns, miners of the green stones, welcomed the forest Orns openly. They no longer mined the stones because they couldn't tell the difference between the stones and the rocks around them. Without the color, they all looked the same.

Pan talked at length with the head of the northern Orns, Robin, an exotic female with dirt-streaked clothes. Because of the loss of contact between the northern Orns and the Goldwood Forest, they knew nothing of the war brewing with King Ro. They attempted to send messengers when the color disappeared but couldn't create a path through the great undergrowth. Pan also learned that very few Warriors existed among them, so their help would not have been great.

The forest Orns lived comfortably among the northern Orns. They lived in the caves, and gathered water and food in the surrounding area. On the fourth day after the fall of Jacob, they saw the Treetop City burn. They watched in silence, many with tears streaming down their cheeks, as the flames engulfed their homes.

Orns began to disappear after going out to gather water and food. They would simply go out of the caves and never come back. It was the fifth day when Alice vanished while gathering water for the Orns. Pan's heart broke as he waited for hours for her to return. He felt as though he'd let Jacob down by not guarding her well enough.

On the sixth day, a scouting party showed themselves too close to the homes of Pan's Orns, so he and the few Warriors he had attacked them. It was a brutal fight, and the Orns were able to vent their frustration, sadness, anger, and boredom through their swords and into the skulls of the king's soldiers.

On the seventh day, early in the morning, Alice returned. Pan's heart leapt as she walked into the cave that morning.

"Where have you been?" he asked her after a quick embrace.

"I was taken by the king's soldiers."

"And you've escaped?"

Alice looked into Pan's eyes, hers still retaining the purple Jacob had restored. "No, Pan, I was rescued."

"Rescued? By who?"

And at that moment, a young man walked into the cave, his clothes in full color. A black cloak wrapped around his body, and a hood pulled up around his face. The cloak looked so much like something made by the Orns to Pan, but he was sure he'd never seen this man before. But as he lifted his hands to pull the hood back, Pan saw something that just couldn't be real.

Chapter 22

Gathering the Rebels

The cave in the Neverise Mountains, although comfortable, was a far cry from the comforts known to the Orns in the Treetop City. Alice missed her home very much, but it was the loss of Jacob that burdened her thoughts. In the days that followed his death, she did her best to enjoy the caves of the mountains, and even made friends with the northern Orns. She stayed busy, and when Orns began to disappear, and supplies began to run low, she took it upon herself to help.

She was careful when she ventured out, and most times, Pan went with her, insisting that he had to watch her for Jacob. The stream only took twenty minutes to reach from the cave, and Alice always watched, always stayed alert, looking out for the soldiers. It was the fifth day after Jacob's death that she left the cave without waiting for Pan to escort her.

She walked along her usual path to the stream, carrying her bucket tightly in her arms. Her eyes darted from left to right, watching for any sign of movement. It was at the stream of water where she got distracted. She usually did, but Pan would snap her back to reality. Without Pan that day, she drifted back to the basin of water in the Treetop City where she and Jacob shared their first kiss.

She sat on the bed of the stream, staring at her reflection, and thinking about the boy who'd died because of her. She was so entranced that she didn't notice the reflection of a soldier appear in the water next to hers.

The soldier grabbed her. She didn't struggle against him, only let him take her, feeling relief that it had finally happened. He bound her hands and blindfolded her and led her away on the back of a horse to be put to the king's work. As the soldier in front of her rode the horse that carried them, she cried a little, but not because she would miss the Neverise Mountains. She only cried because they didn't kill her so she could go on to Elsewhere and be with Jacob once more.

When they reached their destination, they unbound Alice's hands and removed her blindfold. She blinked back the glaring sunlight as her eyes adjusted. She was in a place she didn't recognize. Around her were other Orns with torn clothes, dirty skin and hair, and blood pooling in sores around their body. The other Orns barely took notice of Alice as they worked through their sweat and misery.

"Get to work," one soldier said to her.

"I don't even know what they're doing," Alice said.

Although, while she watched, she understood that they were making blocks. Some Orns were pouring dirt into molds, others poured water over the tops of the dirt. Then they heated the molds over fire, and great blocks came out. They were building something. Alice wasn't sure what just yet.

"The great King Ro needs a new castle. And you're helping him get it," the soldier told her, shoving her in the back. She stumbled forward into another Orn who kept her from falling.

The soldiers walked on, leaving the Orns to their work. As soon as they were gone, Alice turned to thank the Orn who helped her.

"Thank you, I would've fallen if had you not caught me," she said.

"It is no problem, child," the Orn responded.

Alice's heart raced at the thought of remembering this Orn's voice. "Elda, is that you?"

"Yes, dear, it's Elda," the old Orn responded.

Elda had disappeared out of the caves two days before. Pan thought she must have gotten lost and blamed himself for allowing her out of the cave in the first place. She said she just needed air.

"They even have you working here? What about your blindness?"

"It was either work or die."

"Was your prophecy wrong?"

"Prophecies get fulfilled. They're neither wrong nor right. If they get fulfilled, fine, but if not, it just wasn't meant to happen that way," she hesitated before finishing, "but there are rumors."

"Rumors about what?" A couple other Orns stopped their work to gather around Elda as she conversed with Alice. Elda's words rekindled their hopes.

"We hear the stories told by the soldiers at night, when they think we are asleep. They talk about raids at other work camps where Orns and Elves have been freed.

They say a stranger prowls among the land undoing all that King Ro has done."

"Why haven't you been freed?"

"Our camp is among the largest. Working on the king's castle, we are guarded heavily. We will be among the last, if it is true that there is a hero."

"Why are there other work camps?"

"King Ro is building and expanding his reign over all of Toratoga and the unexplored regions to the north and across the seas. He plans to rule it all."

"Hey," one soldier yelled, taking notice of the group of Orns, "back to work."

They split up and began to work, building King Ro's new castle. Alice never worked so hard in her whole life and felt as if her body would just give up. She kept her mind occupied, thinking of the unknown hero Elda had told her about. She birthed a small hope in her chest at the thought of the hero. She knew she would be rescued, and with a gathering of rebels, she would be able to avenge Jacob's death.

The soldiers allowed the Orns to go to sleep well after the sun went down that day. They lay out under the stars with only the clothes on their backs to keep them warm against the cold around them. When Alice saw them all together, the light from the torches illuminating the area, shock overtook her senses as she realized that there were close to six-hundred Orns in that work camp.

At last the torches were put out and the Orns huddled together in the dark to keep warm. Most fell asleep instantly after the long day's work. Alice crawled among the Orns searching for Elda so she could talk to her more. She found her toward the center of the group and lay down beside her.

"Elda, where are we?" she asked.

"Child, I know not. I've been told that far to the north, on a clear day, you can see the remains of our once great city. But without the trees, the landscape looks so different. Even to those who've known this land their whole lives."

"Is there any hope at all for us?"

"If the rumors are true, yes. It seems that there is someone giving hope to the Orns and Elves. And causing fear among King Ro's men."

A sharp wind blew past Alice and a chill shot up her back. She remained quiet for some time, putting together her thoughts. The deep, heavy breathing of the sleeping Orns around her soon filled the night. Sleep threatened to take her, but a sharp noise to her right caught her attention. Something awoke the guards, and they began to move. She could just see their outline in the dull moonlight.

And all at once, it happened. Torches sprang to life all around the Orns' campsite. The soldiers began running in all directions, and the Orns began to wake from their sleep. Then a bright orange light erupted from the north and sent three soldiers flying over the heads of the Orns. Alice suddenly became afraid that she would die.

The Orns around Alice jumped to their feet, and the soldier tried to maintain order, telling them to get back. The screams began from Alice's left, and were answered by screams to her right. Before long, the whole circle of torches screamed a battle cry and the soldiers frenzied. They began running around, stabbing at the torches, or the people holding the torches. The Orns within the circle realized what was going on and began to fight the soldiers. Even without weapons, the sheer number of the Orns helped to defeat the soldiers.

Although Alice couldn't see beyond the gray torchlight, she caught sight of blades hacking at the soldiers near the light. One by one, soldiers fell, clutching at deep wounds and dying on the sand.

Alice continued laying on the ground, unsure of what to do, whether she should run for her life, or if she should stay and fight. Then a man, clad in a long black cloak with the hood pulled up, burst into the circle exactly where the orange light came from. He walked right up to her, and her fears once more overwhelmed her.

She didn't recognize the man, couldn't make out his features in the dim light with his hood shadowing his face so well. He looked powerful and seemed to be in control of the army around the circle of Orns. She waited, staring up at a figure above her, wondering where this mysterious army had come from. Even with Elda's words echoing in her head, she couldn't quite understand what was happening.

The hooded figure offered his left hand to her, but before she could take it, a soldier came up behind him, sword raised. In the second it took Alice to blink, the man pulled his sword with his right hand and thrust it through the soldier. As he replaced the sword, Alice saw only four fingers on that hand.

"Jacob?" she whispered. She remembered light catching his smile under the hood just before she fainted.

Chapter 23

In-Between

At the time of his death, Jacob still held the Anjel's magic inside of his body. The magic, which he pictured as a bright orange, burned in his dead body, wanting to escape. The Odds buried him alongside two other dead Orns. There were no markers on their graves as no one came to visit these dead. They simply provided a place for the bodies to rot while the souls went on to Elsewhere for eternal happiness.

They put Jacob into the ground as unceremoniously as anyone else that died. To the Odds, they were only bodies. Jacob, although a hero in Toratoga, in In-Between, he was only dead. Another body for the Odds to pick and plunder over. They didn't touch his ring; they found no worth in objects of human desire. Their luxuries were in the flesh of the bodies they retrieved. Their deepest desire was for faces. They didn't want to be the faceless Odds so they would take the faces of the dead and wear them as their own until their cursed skulls would rot the flesh.

The young boy's face was among the first they took that day.

They scooped the dirt on the boy's body until the hole in which they'd laid him filled. With no eyelids to close, his eyes filled with dirt, as did his nose, and grains of it fell between his teeth. After the burial, the Odds went about their task of floating over the ground, checking over each grave, showing off their new faces to each other. For them, the Great War of Toratoga was a great time as they got new faces anytime they wanted.

For three days, Jacob stayed dead in the grave, allowing the worms and crawly things found in the dirt to crawl through his flesh. For three days, the Odds went about their business without incident. On that third day, the stone in Jacob's ring changed from green to bright orange. The magic from the Anjel grew more and more powerful until, at last, it was ready to be released.

Bright orange light filled the hole in his chest that King Ro's crooked sword left. The skin around it expanded, covering the wound, until only a small scar remained on Jacob's chest. The magic jolted around and around in Jacob's body and finally stirred him from his deep slumber.

At once, his hand shot up through the dirt, and inch by inch, he dug through the mound that rested on top of him. He didn't know where he was, but he knew he had to get back to the battle. The king might have killed many more by now. He couldn't wait to see Pan and fight alongside him. The captain would surely be shocked to see him, especially since looking into Pan's face was the last thing Jacob could remember.

He dug without considering what he was doing, and all the while, his ring glowed with the bright orange light.

The dirt fell around him, and only a few moments after he'd woken up, his right hand emerged from the dirt. He struggled only a moment before he pulled himself out of the hole, suddenly needing to breathe more than anything else.

He coughed and sprayed the dirt out of his lungs. Without eyelids to hold his eyes in, they fell from their sockets, so that Jacob could only see the ground. He realized that the skin of his face was missing, and suddenly, he knew where he was. He remembered talking to Pan about the blue ladies taking the faces off the corpses.

He lifted his eyes so that he could look around, ignoring the sting from touching the bare eyeball. It looked like any spooky graveyard from movies and TV, without the tombstones. A ground mist rolled gently over the ground and darkness loomed over everything. The occasional blue light floating in the distance told him that the Odds roamed about the ground.

He stuffed his eyes back in their sockets and stole one last glance at his grave. He tried not to look down to keep them from falling out again. The orange color of his stone caught his eye, and he remembered the wound in his chest. He thrust his hand into his shirt and felt for the wound. Only the scar remained.

He walked away from his grave, wondering briefly how many bodies lay under him. A terrible scream broke the silence of the graveyard and the ground mist parted behind him. Before he could react, cold boney hands clinched his arms, the touch chilling his flesh.

"He's alive," he heard a voice say. It wasn't much unlike any woman he'd ever heard before, but there was something in it. Something that forced images of blood and murder into his mind. "This one is alive," it said again.

Jacob turned to look at the Odd that held him. His eyes lit up and anger coursed through his body when he looked back into his own face. The Odd that had taken his face held him firmly, its cold hands almost tearing his flesh. More Odds began to swoop in from around their various places. As Jacob's anger grew, so did the intensity of the stone's light. The orange grew brighter and seemed to scare all shadows away.

The nearest Odd said, "Look at the ring."

The other Odds stopped moving and the grip on Jacob's arm loosened.

"He has the magic of an Anjel," another shrieked.

The Odd holding Jacob let go of his arms and backed away. But not fast enough. Jacob shot out his right hand, the nub of his forefinger extended, and a bright orange finger protruded from the flesh of it. The magic finger made contact with the Odd and it froze. The blue color of its light shifted to the bright orange of the magic. Jacob's face fell from the Odd, and in its place, beautiful flesh began to grow. It crept as slowly as the coming day, and soon Jacob could see the beautiful features of the woman the Odd once was.

He wasted no time in returning the flesh of his face to its rightful place. The bright orange light surrounded it, and almost at once, the light healed his flesh. Horrific scars lined parts of Jacob's face from the flesh being torn from his skull.

The Odd's transformation concluded, and she looked down at herself, admiring the flesh of her hands and arms. "I'm beautiful again. Thank you, Jacob," she said. Her voice was no longer terrible, but songlike and wonderful in such a terrible place. Tears spilled down her cheeks, an odd sight in such a crooked place. The other Odds screamed and formed a circle around Jacob and the former Odd.

"How do we get out of here?" Jacob asked the woman.

"I don't, Jacob, I am cursed. I must stay here." The Odds drew in closer and closer.

"You can't be serious. You have to come with me."

"Leaving here will destroy me."

"Staying here will destroy you."

The screams of the Odds filled the night, and fleshless hands began to spring from the ground around them. The Odds were calling the dead to their aid.

"You have to hurry, Jacob."

"I don't know what to do," he screamed and once more, the stone sparked like orange lightening springing from the sky. He did the only thing he could: he tapped the magic he'd held onto for so long. At once, his feet left the ground.

"Yes, Jacob, that's it, now go." The encouragement came from the changed Odd, but Jacob didn't need it. He could fly, and that was all the encouragement he needed. He reached back and grabbed the lady's hand, already hands of the dead groped around her ankles. He pulled her with him and flew.

"Please, you must let me stay," she screamed at him.

"I couldn't leave you to their mercy."

The Odds sounded a scream that echoed through every chamber of Jacob's head. He flew up over the Odds, pulling the lady with him into the sky.

"You have to go back down. You have to go through one of them to open the gateway out."

Jacob didn't question her; he changed direction and flew back to the group of Odds. Only one stood far out from the group, so he aimed for that one. The Odd raised her arms in an attempt to block Jacob from entering, but his momentum carried him through. His head hit the chest, and instantly, the world turned blue, like he was flying through a great blue cloud. And an instant later, he'd gone through.

A rush of wind blasted past him as he escaped the Odd's body. Pieces of the Odd flew all around him, and the rest of the Odds screamed even louder. But Jacob paid no attention to them. In the darkness of In-Between, a white doorway had opened to reveal the daylight of Toratoga. Jacob flew for it as the rest of the Odds took to the air after him. The orange woman remained in his grip, giving up her fight for him to let her go.

"Hurry! They cannot fly through the gateway unless they are going to collect the dead." Jacob heard the words of the woman and pushed even harder. The wind pelted against him, and water poured out of his eyes. But he reached the gateway first.

He flew through it and into the sky of Toratoga, relishing in the liveliness of the air. His lungs seemed to laugh as the fresh air flowed into them. But before he could celebrate, a very unsettling feeling reached up through his fingertips. He looked back at the orange lady, the Odd he'd changed, and saw that, although her clothes were orange and beautiful, her flesh had turned grey and flaky. As he watched, she began to crumble and blow off into the air, to settle somewhere far away as dust on someone's furniture.

"Thank you for saving me," she managed to say before that too rotted away. Jacob only watched, unable to speak, feeling that he'd caused this. He brought her to her doom; he didn't save her.

After only a moment, she was gone entirely except for the orange dress she wore. It hung on the wind like a flag being flown at half mast on a day of mourning. Jacob hovered, watching the orange fabric float away. He wiped the tears away and turned to face Toratoga and the great black castle rising out of the land.

Chapter 24

A Fine Day for a Rebellion

The sunlight twinkled down from the sky and Alice blinked back the brilliance of it. As she opened her eyes, she realized that the grey sunlight seemed brighter somehow. Something seemed strange to her, the air almost felt different as the sunlight fell in patches around her. Everything felt so familiar, like she'd come home. As her sleep wore off, she remembered the previous night.

She sat up, her excitement building with the memories. She'd seen him, she was almost sure of it. He'd come back, somehow, and he'd rescued her. She stood to her feet but didn't know where to go to begin looking for him. Then she realized she stood under a tree.

Her eyes widened and her lips parted ever so slightly as she stared up at the tree above her. Her hand reached to feel the familiar surface of the bark. Her eyes darted from the deep golden roots up to the great branches covered in silver leaves. She blinked and tears fell freely down her cheeks. She let them come, only wanting to stand there, getting her fill of the tree in front of her. The pain of watching the Treetop City burn leaked out with each tear. Jacob came to save them and, as far as she was concerned in that moment, he'd achieved it.

Her hand still caressed the golden bark even as Jacob walked up behind her. His black cloak removed for the meeting, he approached her nervously. As she felt his presence, she turned toward him, and their eyes, his green, hers violet, met. She took in all of him, like a long drink after a hot day.

Little red scars decorated his skin around the eyes and chin. He looked the same, only slightly distorted. He reached out his hand to her, his right hand, and she couldn't help but look for the missing finger. With that, there was no doubt that Jacob Nine-fingers, who died on the battlefield at the hands of King Ro, now stood before her.

She placed her hand into his, and he brought her to him. They embraced, allowing no trace of sunlight to filter between them. Beautiful magic sprung out from around them, and the tree they stood under shot another thirty feet into the air. Grass sprang up around their feet, thick green grass. And the first bird heard in Toratoga since the evil broke free sang its song high above them in the branches of the golden tree.

Jacob and Alice noticed none of this, however, only enjoying the warmth of each other's embrace. For Alice the meeting seemed unreal, like a beautiful dream, and her tears soaked into Jacob's shoulder. For Jacob the reunion was perfect. He'd been back only three days, but all of those days were too long without Alice.

At long last, their embrace ended. Jacob smiled as he wiped away the remaining tears from Alice's face. She giggled and looked into his eyes.

"Oh, Jacob," she said, her voice barely more than a whisper, "I thought you were gone."

"I was gone, Alice. But I'm back."

"It's all my fault. You should never have come here."

"No, if you wouldn't have brought me here, I wouldn't have you. These things happen for a reason, Alice."

Before Alice could respond, an Orn interrupted them. "Sir," said the Orn, "we should move to the Neverise Mountains. I'm afraid your tree may have brought some unwanted attention."

Jacob looked from the warrior to the tree above him and smiled. "Ah, yes," he said, "and, Alice, where is my captain?"

"Pan is in the Neverise Mountains. Many of us took refuge there. I was among them before the king captured me."

"And how did he capture you?"

"Your memory snuck up on me."

Jacob laughed at the simple explanation Alice gave him. She watched in awe as orange sparks flew forth from his mouth with each burst of laughter.

"We should be off," he said. "Let's journey to the north."

Jacob led the Orns, Elves, and the few human rebels to the mountains in the north part of Toratoga. Alice saw that Jacob had been busy since he'd returned from In-Between. Hundreds of her kin had been set free by him but he'd only assembled half of the army. As they marched northward, she felt her heart flutter at the thought of freedom.

They reached the foot of the mountains a few hours after nightfall. They rested for the evening before continuing on to the caves where Pan and the rest of the Orns lived in hiding. Somewhere behind them, stood that lone tree, a relic of the Goldwood Forest and a telling of the things to come.

Alice rushed into the cave fist to meet Pan. He grabbed her up in a tight embrace, surprised to see her again. But it was when Jacob entered and revealed himself that Pan believed his mind played tricks on him.

"Pan, captain of the Orn Warriors, will you lead the army of the Orns in battle once more?" Jacob asked after he lowered the hood of his cloak.

"Jacob, is it really you?" Pan stammered, his eyes wide and still unbelieving.

"Yes, of course. And it's time you and your people were freed from the tyranny of King Ro. It's time for rebellion."

"But how? How is any of this possible?"

"Don't you believe, Pan? The power to wield the magic of this world was once available to you and you doubt me being here?"

"No. Well, I don't understand any of it. I could use magic, but I never thought any of the powers you've possessed would be possible. And what about the army? We have none."

"Have a look outside before you go on assuming."

Pan's eyes darted from Alice to Jacob and, hesitating only slightly, he walked past the risen child and out of the cave entrance. The crowd of Orns erupted at the sight of their captain, and tears sprang forth from Pan's eyes. The familiar faces and people overwhelmed him.

"They're yours to lead once more," Jacob whispered as he came up next to Pan.

Pan tore his eyes from the crowd to Jacob. "No, they're yours. You've freed them. You've earned the right to be their captain."

"I have other matters to attend to." He slipped his hand down to his tunic and lifted it to reveal the puckered red scar tissue where the king's sword pierced him. The attack that killed him.

Pan took one look at it and understood everything. This wasn't just about saving Toratoga anymore. This was revenge for putting Jacob through death.

"Our numbers are smaller than that of the first battle, but so are King Ro's. We've taken several of his soldiers, and he's noticed. He almost overtook us. The trees are coming back."

Pan listened intently, but his eyes brightened at the last words Jacob said. "They're coming back?" He looked to Alice who nodded in confirmation and whose own eyes began to tear up once more at the mention of the trees.

"The evil is losing its stronghold. We are on the downside of the reign of King Ro. Now, we rest, and in the morning, we march. You will lead the troops to the south, and King Ro will meet you once more on the deserted plains."

"Will you not march with us?"

"I will catch up with you, I promise. I just have one thing to attend to before I join you."

He nodded. "Then tonight, we feast."

As the sun descended, the Orns and Elves fellowshipped with food and drink. The Northern Orns showed their brethren immense hospitality. Jacob walked among the Orns, stopping to meet a few and listen to stories of others. But his focus that night was Alice.

The two of them walked hand in hand, showing the pride of their love. Jacob felt complete, the urgency of the looming battle held at bay by the presence of his Alice. Somehow, the only thing that mattered to him that night was the presence of Alice. And she felt quite the same way.

Slowly, the Orns and Elves let sleep overtake them. The battle ahead of them seemed foolish since the return of Jacob Nine-fingers. Their minds were at ease, and their bellies full. Jacob watched as each one fell asleep where they sat.

As last, he helped Alice into a bed inside the caves. She slept heavily, not noticing the kiss Jacob placed on her lips. She didn't even notice as he said goodbye and slipped from the cave, and left the Neverise Mountains. No other Orn saw Jacob leave that night, but instead, they slept the peaceful sleep of the dead.

Jacob walked on through the night to collect his army. An army fit for the downfall of a king.

Chapter 25

The Fall

The sun withdrew from the horizon, casting its gray light, gray but not as dull, across the land. It glanced and broke into a thousand pieces as it hit the dew on the grass. Little by little, the rays reached the sleeping Warriors at the foot of the Neverise Mountains. One by one, the Orns blinked it back, but let the morning welcome them. They all knew what the day would bring.

Pan quickly organized the Warriors into his army once more, falling back into the role of Captain very easily. The Orn women stayed behind, expecting their men to return from this battle. Alice and Elda wished Pan the best as he set the Warriors marching.

Although the absence of Jacob troubled her, Alice found strength in the memory of him coming to save her. He didn't abandon her then, and he wouldn't now. She was sure.

But as the army marched, the Warriors began to notice the absence of the child hero. They began to talk about it among themselves, which Pan did his best to ignore, until one Orn voiced the concern of the whole army.

"Where is Jacob Nine-fingers?" the Warrior asked.

The army erupted with him. Everyone felt the pressure of not having Jacob with them, and they wanted answers.

Pan stopped walking and turned to face his Warriors. "You want to know where Jacob is?"

"Yeah," they shouted.

"Don't you see what this is? This is liberation. This is facing the greatest tyranny in the whole history of our world. This is our chance for freedom, the freedom we once enjoyed together in our Treetop City. Yes, we march without the child hero from the prophecy, but we march as the greatest army Toratoga has ever seen.

"Grebbles and humans alike will tremble before our power. We will conquer King Ro, and we will restore good in our land. Look out before you, as far as your eye can see, and find the trees. They are growing once more, returning from the sand of this vast desert.

"Today, fellow Orns and Elves, we march on the black castle, and we end this war. Look not for Jacob, but for the courage in your own hearts. For the desire to see your homes restored."

The army grew quiet, and Pan led them on. A distinct feeling of foreboding fell over the troops as they thought on Pan's words. He didn't mention anything about Jacob joining them in combat. That thought alone frightened them.

But they marched on. Every last one of them, each carrying a sword that would soon drip with the blood of the enemy. As the sun rose in the sky, their hearts lightened, until they saw the king's army riding toward them. A great black mass unfolding in the distance.

King Ro sent his army the night before, so they'd gained much more ground than the Orns had expected. They would meet in a couple of short hours. If it wasn't for the sighting of trees, the army probably would have fled before the king. But the trees, their former homes, reminded them of what was lost.

They stood, only a few of them, off to the east of the king's army. Even from the distance, they could see the gold of the bark glimmering in the sunlight, and the silver of the leaves catching the rays and casting them in different directions.

Onward they marched; Pan, the fearless captain, leading the Warriors to the final battle against King Ro's foes. Only two hours after spotting the king's army, they drew close enough to create a battlefield between them. King Ro rode to the front of his army on his great black steed, his face now entirely covered in the black vine tattoo, giving him a more malicious look than ever.

"Even now you defy me, Pan," the king shouted.

"It is your time, Ro. Throw off your crown and give up the kingdom."

"Such demands from a dying race. You may have managed to free a few of your kind, but the power still resides with me."

"'Twas not I who freed the Orns, Ro, but your fallen enemy."

King Ro looked back over his shoulder at his army, the blue skin of the Grebbles glazing beautifully in the falling sunlight. He faced Pan and his army once more. "What nonsense are you speaking of now, Pan?"

"Not nonsense, only truth. The boy you killed, for he did indeed die, returned to Toratoga to right the wrong you've put upon this land. He's freed us from your slavery, and he will free us from your tyranny."

"And yet, Pan, I look among your numbers and I see no signs of the boy. If he has indeed returned, as you say, why then does he not show himself?"

Jacob had gone off to gather more magic than he'd ever carried, and to find Elea, the Anjel who helped him in the first battle. When he found the Anjel, he looked different. The white blade he'd used on the Uruk Taki no longer shown with the intensity of the heavens.

"I am no longer welcome in the Colors Beyond because of my involvement in your world," Elea told Jacob when he asked about it. "Toratoga is my home now, and I will fight for it."

When King Ro spoke of Jacob showing himself, a great blaze lit the battlefield to the west. In it stood Jacob Nine-fingers, wearing his black cloak with the hood pulled over his head. Elea stood next to him, his wings expanded behind them. The king saw the boy and recognized him at once. His eyebrows arched and his eyes widened.

"How is this possible?" the king whispered, but none aside from his great horse heard. He rode back into formation and spoke to his captain. "Attack," he said. "Aim your arrows at the boy."

The captain could not look King Ro in the eye, but the absurdity of his demand struck him. "But, sir, our arrows would do more damage against the army."

"Do as I say or you will join the dead today." And without another word, the king road back into the throng of his army. The captain stood speechless for a moment

240

before directing his archers to focus only on the boy. The king's army charged once more on the army of the rebels, although the sight of Jacob shook their confidence, and the archers loosed their first group of arrows.

The Orns charged into the king's army, their confidence renewed at the sight of their hero. The arrows stopped in the air before they found their target. Jacob merely flicked his wrist, and the arrows turned back on their owners, killing them all. Elea rushed forward into the din, and Jacob watched as his white blade turned crimson.

He stood still only for a moment. He wanted the war for Toratoga to be over, and he knew the only way was for King Ro to fall. And he was the only one who could kill the once good and great king.

He ran into battle, sword drawn, and faced the enemies of peace and freedom. His sword flew swift and sure. Enemies fell before him, and many scattered in his wake. Around him, Orn Warriors fought with an intensity that drove the king's army back.

Jacob fought through them, finding the opening he'd been seeking. He slipped between many of the fighting soldiers, most of whom did not want to face him anyway, and he searched for the hidden king. He walked through the battle, killing when he must, until the king broadsided him with his own body. He knocked the unaware Jacob to the ground.

Jacob stood quickly and faced the king. "Your power over this world is failing," Jacob said. "Already the trees return and color returns to everything. Look at the blood on my blade."

"All I have to do is kill you and my hold on this world will return," the king answered, as he pulled his own blade from its sheath.

"And how many more times will you kill me? You die today, Ro."

"No, you die, and you stay dead."

His voice rose to a scream that rippled Jacob's clothing and his flesh. He pulled a handful of white dust from the inside of his cloak that Jacob recognized at once as the ash from the burnt Orns. He held it to his nose and, in one breath, he sucked it all up.

And as Jacob watched, the king's eyes turned completely black and overflowed their boundaries like slick black tears. The black vines that decorated the king's face, and spread throughout his body like some terrible plague, ripped free from the flesh of his face, tearing the skin off with it. The black vines surrounded his bloody skull like some menacing snakes. His black eyes spilled over more, streaking his white, fleshless skull with black.

Horror spread through Jacob as he watched the king's transformation. Evil completely overtook, and somehow, Jacob felt like a thirteen-year old boy again, afraid of what might be in the closet or under the bed. For a moment, his courage failed, and he turned, ever so slightly, to flee away from the demented king of Toratoga. But as he turned, his eye caught a small portion of the battle. In that instant he saw the Orns beating back the enemy. If the Orns won, they would still be ruled by this evil, and Jacob knew he was the only one able to stop it.

Jacob faced his fears once more. Looking at the black and white skull of the king, he faced every spider, every snake, every nightmare, and everything that caused him to hide under the safety of his blankets in bed. He pulled every ounce of courage he could find, and he stood face to face with King Ro for the final time.

The king laughed. It was a dark, mirthless sound. "Jacob, you are still here," he said, his voice coming from deep inside that skull. "Should we finish this then?"

Jacob let the air leave his lungs, the blade of his sword glinting in the grey sunlight. Before he could draw another breath, he ran toward the king. Despite feeling more fear than he'd felt in all his thirteen years, he ran toward the king. He faced his fears because even dying would be better than living and knowing he'd failed to rescue this world.

Their swords met with a resounding crack that echoed through the battlefield. The wild vine tattoos caught hold of Jacob's arm and tore at his flesh. His sword sliced through them, and they fell to the ground as ash. King Ro screamed in outrage and pain when Jacob robbed him of his vines.

He pushed Jacob away from him and put the index finger of his left hand to his blade. At once, a black flame lit the sword's surface without harming the blade. Jacob felt the heat from it and couldn't believe the power the king had achieved.

"Is this why you've not brought any of your Uruk Taki?" Jacob asked him.

"Why would I need those senseless monsters when I have delved deeper into black magic than anyone before me? I am more powerful than even the Anjels."

"Your pride is truly dizzying."

The king lunged this time, but not before Jacob could light his own blade with an orange flame from the last of the Anjel's magic. Once more, their swords met.

The flames entwined around each other and shot high in the sky as the king and Jacob stared at each other over their blades.

"Give it up, boy," the king said.

In response, Jacob lifted his right hand from the hilt of his sword and pointed his stub at the king. Before the king could prepare his defense, green light erupted from Jacob's hand and hit King Ro solidly in the chest. The magic launched the king twenty feet away from Jacob, but he was up again and running toward Jacob almost as soon as he hit the ground.

Jacob acted quickly, launching himself into the air with his magic, and the king followed suit, launching himself up to meet Jacob using his black magic. Once more, the two met. Their swords blazed faster than the eye could perceive in a blast of quick blows, each parried by the other's defenses. They fought furiously, slowly sinking back to land as they did; their magic spells flying out in all directions, never finding their mark.

Although Jacob's strength had increased, his muscles began to ache after fighting against the more powerful King Ro, and the king showed no signs of weakening. Still he fought, but his hope began to fail. As the king took control of the offense, Jacob watched his sword fly out to block the blows, but his thoughts were elsewhere.

He thought of his mother, how he missed her despite his rebellion to her demands. He thought of coming to Toratoga to save the world, a mission that it seemed he would fail. But mostly, he thought of Alice. Her sweet face and violet eyes. Every thought of her made his insides tingle. With those thoughts, the stone of his ring began to turn a rich red like wild roses. And as he thought of the first time he saw her in the backyard of the old house back in Oklahoma, the color of the ring brightened to the point that it spilled out, extinguished the orange flame and outlined the blade of his sword in red.

While his mind continued to wander over the curves of Alice's cheeks, and how light she felt every time she hugged him, his strength returned to his arm and his sword flew out to meet King Ro's with more intensity. He fought harder and faster as each memory of Alice danced through his mind.

The king fell back into defense without even realizing that the tide had turned. Jacob's arms seemed to vanish as they flew through the air, seeking their mark. The whites of Jacob's eyes turned up as he lost himself in the memory of his first and only love. King Ro's strength began to fail, until at last, it was gone entirely.

He fell to his knees before Jacob, holding out his sword to block the never ending blows of Jacob's sword. And then, King Ro's sword broke. The snap of the metal echoed throughout the battlefield, bringing everything to a halt and pulling Jacob out of his trance. The color of his eyes rolled back, and he looked down at the king.

Ro sat on his knees, panting, the black vines sinking back into his face, and his flesh growing back. He looked up into Jacob's eyes, and Jacob felt pity on him. He tucked his sword back into its sheath.

"Leave here," he said. "Give up your throne, and be gone with you. Torment some place other than these lands."

Ro slowed his panting and watched Jacob, amazed. Jacob shook his head, and turned away from Ro, walking slowly as the wind whipped his black cloak around his legs. The battle remained halted, and everyone watched Jacob walk away from the defeated king. Some thought the boy valiant. Others thought him a worthless hero.

Each of Jacob's steps brought the armies to a closer realization that the war was over. An overwhelming surge of relief washed over him as he walked, until he heard his name. It came to him like he slowly woke from a deep sleep. But each time he heard it, his head cleared. He looked in the direction from which it came and saw Alice running toward him. Beautiful Alice. He saw the panic in her face and the frenzied pace with which she ran.

"Jacob, behind you!" she screamed again, this time fully breaking the cloud around Jacob's mind. He turned but too late.

Ro came from behind him, holding the jagged hilt of his broken sword. Madness streaming from his eyes like tears. He buried the broken sword up to the hilt in Jacob's side. Jacob looked at Ro then down at the hilt protruding from his side. He stood very still for a moment, feeling the metal once more embedded where it shouldn't be. In the twitter of a fly's wing, he pulled his own sword from its sheath and forced it into Ro's chest. The king's insane grin froze on his face as he watched his blood, a deep red, flow from his body.

Before Jacob could react further, she was there. Alice stood by his side, the flesh of her fingers caressing the flesh of his face. He fell to his knees just as Ro fell to his. Alice knelt beside Jacob, whispering her love for him in his ear. His eyes wandered from the dying king to Alice, her violet eyes locking on his green ones, keeping them there. He smiled and she smiled. And all at once, he couldn't hold anything back.

Magic like red light shot out from his mouth and eyes like violent vomit during a bad flu. Jacob screamed, but felt no pain, only love. The love he felt for Alice. The buried hilt shot out of his body and red magic poured from the hole, mingling with the blood. Jacob looked back at Ro as the red magic surrounded him. Ro screamed in pain as the magic pouring from Jacob faded, and the magic surrounding Ro devoured him. A small sonic boom lit the air as the magic closed in around him, then vanished. The boom knocked over everyone on the field.

And King Ro was gone.

†

That night, the land of Toratoga celebrated. The color fully returned, and the trees shot out from the ground, giving the land its former glory. Evil left the land, and the Grebbles were once more forced to the East. Even the humans celebrated the downfall of King Ro as if the king had a spell over them that broke only when he died.

Alice checked Jacob's wound that the red magic had healed entirely, and the two of them found a quiet area away from all the celebrations.

"You came to the battlefield. But why?" Jacob asked.

"I couldn't bear to not be here in case something happened to you again. I snuck away from the other Orn women."

"You helped me escape death for the second time. Without you, Toratoga would be lost."

"You're the hero, Jacob."

"Only because you believed in me."

"You could have done it without me."

"But I never would have come had it not been for you coming to that house." A troubled expression fell over Jacob's features.

"What is it?" Alice asked quietly.

"The house. The old house at the end of Ash Street. I can't believe I didn't think of it sooner, but where is Mr. Hansen? He found the bathtub and disappeared, he has to be here."

Alice sat up, staring at Jacob. "He is here. When he entered Toratoga three years ago, the Orns welcomed him, until the downfall of King Ro and the apparent downfall of Galadawn. That's when the Tribesmen had him arrested and sent to the East."

"The East?" Jacob thought for a moment. "But that means there are still prisoners there. We must save them."

"We will, Jacob, but not tonight."

Alice rested her head on Jacob's shoulder and his mind began to ease back from the thoughts of the prisoners. Jacob's mind returned to his triumph on the battlefield and how Alice had saved him. He had to tell her how he felt.

They sat quiet for a moment while Jacob mustered up the courage to tell her how she helped him.

"Alice, I love you." The heat rushed up to his cheeks. He'd never told anyone outside of his parent's that he loved them.

"Jacob, I know, and I love you."

She fell into his arms, careful not to hurt his aching body, and she kissed him. Red sparks lit up around them as their love overflowed into the atmosphere of Toratoga.

Epilogue

Jacob Kepler once again stood on Ash Street in Abbey, Oklahoma. He stood outside of the giant house at the end of the street, staring at the other end, toward his home. He'd come out through the black bathtub, just as he'd entered into that world. He wouldn't go back that way, there was no need now. Now that his ring had been fixed.

Jacob took one last look back at the house. The new owners stood on the porch still looking at him very strangely. He'd somehow convinced them not to call the police, even though he looked like a wild man.

His shoulder length hair blew back in the wind as he walked down Ash Street. He found his courage lacking as he thought of seeing his mother for the first time in four years. He looked down at his right hand where the green glove hid his missing finger from view. He walked lightly down the road, feeling the asphalt through his golden shoes. His well-worn cloak hung around him, keeping him a little too warm for an early fall day in Oklahoma.

"I must look a lot like Alice did when she first came to see me," Jacob thought. He smiled. Thoughts of Alice always made him smile.

At long last, Jacob reached the yellow house where he'd last seen his mother. He had no idea if she still lived there or not, but he had to at least find out. He walked up to the front door with a fear he hadn't felt in years and convinced himself to ring the doorbell. He heard footsteps on the other side and the door opened.

"Yes?" his mother said, staring at the strange looking person standing on her front porch.

"I was passing through town and I felt a bit weary. I wonder if I could come in and have a rest," Jacob said. His mother obviously was unsure of how to treat this stranger on her porch, but something in his eyes made him seem safe. She nodded and opened the door.

Jacob walked into the house. Not much had changed over the last few years. He took in the smell and remembered his mother. Sometimes when he was a small boy, when his parents were still together, she would put on the sweetest smelling perfume. No one else ever wore it and that smell always brought his mother back to his mind.

He sat on the couch and looked at her.

"I'm sorry that my husband isn't here. He's off being the mayor," she said.

Jacob perked up at her words, thinking longingly that his parents had gotten back together and his father had become mayor of Abbey. But then he remembered the fat man he'd met shortly after moving into this house. He cast his eyes around and found their wedding photos. Sure enough, there stood Boss holding onto his mother's hand.

Can I get you a drink or something to eat?" she asked.

"No, thank you," Jacob replied. "Just some company would be fine."

"All right," she said as she sat on the couch across from him.

"Do you like it here in Abbey?" he asked.

"Yes, it took a while, but I do like it now. Some things just need adjusting. After I remarried, that helped quiet down my life."

"When did you move here?"

"Four years ago, I think. Yes, it really has been that long." She had a gleam in her eye thinking about those early days.

"Do you have any children?"

"What?" she asked, coming back to reality. "Yes, I have, um, I have one child. He lives with his father three blocks north of here."

"Your son lives here?" Once more Jacob found himself surprised by the circumstances of the last four years.

"Yes, well, they didn't always. Shortly after I moved here my other son disappeared, and they moved here to help me find him. His father seemed the most upset by it all and insisted on coming."

"What was his name, the other child?"

"Jacob. His name was Jacob."

Jacob looked intently at his mother and saw the worry etched on her face, moisture welling up in her eyes. He saw what the last four years without him had done to her. He saw that it was his absence that led to her marrying the overweight "Boss."

He stood, crossed the room, and knelt in front of her.

"I am sorry," he said.

"No, no, there is no need for that, it was a long..."

She stopped short and stared at Jacob. She looked at his face, the scars were deep in some places and made him look years older than he was. She looked at his ears that he decorated with the jewelry of the Orn people. And finally, she looked into his eyes, and the green of them washed away the scars, the years, everything. She could see her thirteen-year-old son.

"Jacob?" she said.

"Yes, Mom, it's me," he said.

"But where...why...I don't understand," she managed.

"I've been to Toratoga, Mom. I had to go to save their world. And I have to go back."

"No, you've only just got here," she said.

"I came to make sure you were all right. I came to see if you wanted to return with me."

"Return with you?" she asked.

"Yes, Mom, come back to Toratoga with me, it can be a new beginning for you."

She saw in his eyes the seriousness of the request and at once made up her mind to go. She suddenly forgot about her life in Abbey, forgot about her husband and became completely lost in the return of her son. "I should call your father, let him know that you're all right."

"No, Mom, we'll leave a note for Dad, I've already written it. He'll understand. And if he wants to come, he'll find a way." She nodded at his words, although she still looked very confused.

Jacob went to the bathroom and filled the bathtub with water, preparing it for their journey to Toratoga, to his world.

When Taylor came by two hours later to check on his mother, he found an empty house. He looked around, but he couldn't find his mother anywhere. There was only a bathtub full of water and a rolled up parchment of golden paper.

Taylor unrolled it.

Beautiful silver words decorated the page. It surprised him to see his name written on the parchment.

"Jacob," he whispered as he began to read the letter.

Dad and Taylor,

I am sorry that I've been away for all these years, but I came back to tell you that I am all right, and that I can't stay. I've taken Mom with me, so don't worry about her. I really hope to see you two again, so, Dad, if you want to come, there's a way in the attic at the end of Ash Street.

Love Always,
Jacob

Taylor sat in silence staring at the letter. Then he rolled it back up and, taking one last look around, headed out the door to ask his dad about the mysterious disappearance of his brother and mom.

About the Author

Nick Lyon is a native of Alva, Oklahoma, a member of the Oklahoma Writer's Federation, Inc., and a member of the Red Dirt Writer's Society. He is also the author of the short story collection *It'll All Work Out*. When not writing, he spends his time teaching English, walking his dogs, Jake and Jandy, spending time with his girlfriend Ashley, and playing with his band, The Dead Armadillos. He currently resides in Oklahoma City.